Sherlock Holmes: The Long Game

Angel, Saints, and Sinners series

William David Ellis

Altar Stone Publishing

William David Ellis/ Altar Stone Publishing
Mineola, Texas, USA, 75773
www.williamdavidellisauthor@yahoo.com

Publisher's Note: This is a work of fiction. Names, characters, places, and incidents are a product of the author's imagination. Locales and public names are sometimes used for atmospheric purposes. Any resemblance to actual people, living or dead, or to businesses, companies, events, institutions, or locales is completely coincidental.

Book Layout © 2017 BookDesignTemplates.com

Sherlock Holmes: The Long Game, Book #2 in Angels, Saints and Sinners series. William David Ellis. -- 1st ed.
ISBN 978-1-7338850-6-5

CONTENTS

The Long Game

Francis Alparts played on the floor of Sherlock Holmes' apartment with his six-month-old child. Jonnie, his wife, enjoyed the moment and rested her tired eyes, or so she said. John Watson, who couldn't help but cast a physician's keen gaze on her sleeping face, chuckled as the feather loosely attached to her fashionable straw bonnet shivered beneath her soft exhalations. The night was late, and it looked like the Alparts family would be staying over for the evening. It was a recurring habit, one with which everyone was very comfortable, and it had been going on for months.

Holmes was busy puffing on his pipe and reading an ancient vellum manuscript from the latter part of the fifteenth century on the fine art of healing herbs and poisons.

The Alparts family had adopted Holmes and Watson and treated them like favored uncles. At first, Holmes had been distant and aloof, but time and almost daily exposure had caused him to love their child, whom they promptly tried to name Holmes Watson Alparts. Sherlock objected strongly, saying that the boy should be named after his father and not some wayfaring stranger who just happened to drift upon their shores.

So, they debated. Everyone had his favorite names, and all were considered, some given more consideration than others. No one liked Dr. Watson's contribution of Wrick, or Sherlock's favorite, Alroy. Jonnie tried to pacify everyone by combining Francis' desire to name the child after Sherlock with Watson's favorite, Wrick, and came up with Shrek. At first the name seemed to stick; then Holmes said he had, on good authority—as the only one who had traveled into the future—that although Shrek was a good name, it probably was not the one they should use for their child. So, they went back to the drawing board.

Finally, after Teddy, Bundy, Adolf, John Wilkes, Jesse, Dahmer, and Osama had been rejected, Francis put his large foot down and said if they did not come to a conclusion soon, he would just call the child *Boy* and be done with it. Of course, that caused Jonnie to burst into tears, Holmes to walk away in a cloud of pipe smoke, and Watson to retire to his scotch. After a few hours, Jonnie came back and, in a very tentative manner, suggested they call the child Robert Francis Sheriton Alparts. For a long moment, every eye searched every other eye and somber face for consensus, and then the deed was done. Thus, they proceeded to call the baby Bob and were done with it.

Gathered as a typical English extended family, laughing, smoking, drooling, and snoring, they were not expecting a sharp rap on the apartment door.

Before the second knock had finished sounding, Sherlock stood frowning, Jonnie grabbed the baby and hustled toward the back bedroom, Watson put down his drink, and Francis stood to reach for the door.

Holmes stopped Francis by placing his hand on the giant's arm. He whispered, "Did you hear anyone ascend the stairs?"

Francis shook his head.

"Neither did I, and it is certainly not like Mrs. Hudson to allow an uninvited guest inside. Something is wrong. Stand aside, please." Holmes motioned for the huge bulk of a man to move discreetly behind him, then added, "But be ready should I need you."

Francis nodded and set his jaw. His eyes turned cold as he curled his fists, the size of small bowling balls.

A third knock was met by Holmes slowly opening the door and peering out. A middle-aged man with dark hair and a short-boxed beard stood in the hall. He was tall and immaculately dressed in a close-fitting shirt with cuffed sleeves and a high collar. His trousers, held by a pair of elastic suspenders, fell loosely to his ankle and were accessorized with a top hat and an Inverness cape. Overall, he was the picture of aristocratic English wealth. There were only two problems: Firstly, he was soaking wet. Water ran from his clothes and pooled around the edges of his narrow-toed boots. Secondly, a large knife protruded from a bloody wound in the center of his chest.

Holmes jerked back as Francis jumped between him and the man standing in the hall. No one moved. Finally, the visitor sighed and spoke. "I am here to inquire as to the consulting service of one Sherlock Holmes. Is he available?"

Holmes recovered slowly, his heart still beating wildly, but he was able to speak. He gently motioned Francis to one side and answered, "I am he. How may I help you?"

The man stared, still in the hallway, waiting for an invitation. Holmes did not offer it. The man's eyebrows rose, but Holmes didn't respond. Francis' face twitched and his fist tightened. The man sighed again and continued, "It is customary for a gentleman to be invited inside before discussing matters of business, is it not, Mr. Holmes?"

Holmes stared back, and after a second's pause, "It is. But are you a gentleman? Many strangers and stranger yet have recently knocked at my door. I have come to realize a threshold is a barrier to some of the more dangerous beings that haunt the night, so, sir, on your honor—and I am sure you can see my associate is more than able to ensure that honor"—he turned to Francis with a grateful nod, then back to the stranger—"do you give me your word that you do not mean me nor anyone behind my doors harm?"

The man frowned and huffed, "Of course I do, sir! Of course! Now may I come in?"

Holmes backed away from the door. "Yes, please be seated." He pointed to an ornate wicker rocker that Watson typically set aside for guests to use. It was waterproof, and in this case, perfect.

Watson had seen only Holmes' and Francis' reactions to the stranger but was experienced enough to have reached for his short-barreled shotgun and now held it to his side. The gun was loaded with silver-laced shells. He started to ask, "Would you like some..." but halted when he saw the water-soaked condition and the huge knife sticking out from the stranger's chest. Wide-eyed and mouth agape, he stood speechless till Francis nudged him. He shook his head vigorously, blinked, and tried to continue, "Tea, sir?"

The man laughed. "I wish, sir, but considering my current condition, I'm not sure where I would store it, much less get it down. So, thank you kindly, but no." Then turning to Holmes, "I would like to consult with you, Mr. Holmes, if this is not too much of an intrusion?"

Jonnie walked back into the room, having put Bob down for the night. Upon surveying the stranger, she stopped short, her eyes widened, and her posture straightened. She had not gasped, nor her heart surged, but she was coiled like a pantheress ready to spring. A protruding knife in someone's chest had a way of causing that kind of reaction.

Holmes swept the room with his hand. "These are my able and talented associates. They are professional and very gifted in dealing with things that... based on your appearance," he nodded toward the large knife in the man's chest, "you might have need of."

The man followed Holmes' gaze and stared at the knife as if he had forgotten it was there. "Oh yes, yes indeed. Well, perhaps introductions are in order. I am Adam Blund, and I ah... would like for you to solve," he hesitated, then forced the words out in a huff, "my murder."

Holmes sat back in his chair; his eyes riveted on Adam Blund. He crossed his long legs as if he had all the time in the world and a man wasn't seated across from him who might or might not be a ghost. Picking up his pipe, he lit it and blew rolling clouds of tobacco upward. Finally, after an awkward and tedious visual examination that had Watson's eyes rolling, Francis' teeth gritting, and Jonnie about ready to shake him, Holmes asked, "Mr. Blund, are you indeed dead?"

Watson cried, "Holmes! For God's sake, man! He has a knife sticking through his chest. He's not bleeding, and he is as pale as a sheet!"

Jonnie murmured, "Mr. Holmes, I have to agree with Dr. Watson. I think Mr. Blund is definitely not among the living. I detect no heartbeat, no respiration, and," she looked to the man for permission; he nodded, so she brushed her index finger across his hand, "his skin is cold and clammy."

Watson interrupted, "Ectoplasm is never very warm, my dear, and I am fairly sure what we see before us is not the original housing of Mr. Blund but his manifested image: solid, wet even, but not actual flesh."

Francis turned to Adam Blund, narrowing his eyes to a fine point. "What happened to you, Mr. Blund? We don't mean to pry, but it's not every day that someone with a knife sticking out of their chest and with the smell of rot on their breath knocks on Mr. Holmes' door to ask for help."

Before Blund could answer, Holmes hypothesized, "You are under a curse, are you not? And, by the looks of things and based on the literature I have studied, you cannot pass on until the curse is broken and the aggrieved party satisfied."

Blund's pale eyes fluttered. He nodded vigorously and whispered, "Yes! Oh yes, Mr. Holmes. I knew I made the right decision to manifest at your door. Can you help me? Oh, please, sir, help me!" Grief overcame the man as heart-wrenching sobs broke over him. He bent beneath them, head in hands, weeping.

Jonnie Alparts, ever the compassionate one, sat beside him and placed her arm around him, heedless of his soaked condition. She handed him a kerchief and, with a great snort, he blew out his consternation, finally settling into an interrogable frame of mind.

Holmes began again. "Mr. Blund, I shall have to ask you some..." He paused for the right word. *Awkward? Disturbing? Troubling even.* "Questions. Please excuse me beforehand and do your best to answer."

"Yes, of course."

Holmes nodded to both Watson and Jonnie, who had taken on the role of his transcribers. What one missed, the other inevitably recorded. Between the two, they made an amazing transcription team.

"When did the incident in question take place?"

Blund tilted his head, confused.

Francis blurted out, "When did you get the knife stuck in you, man!"

"Oh yes, rather... I, ah... hmmmm. Seems like yesterday. There was a blow to my head and a sharp pain in my chest before everything went dark. I woke up on the bottom of the Thames with a huge anchor tied to my feet. I remember seeing a light and moving upward toward it. My head broke the top of the water, and I just barely missed getting hit by a passing barge. Then I saw the shore was close and swam toward it. But since I don't know what day it is, I can't tell you how long ago I was... I was..."

Francis offered, "Murdered? Killed? Done in?"

Blund's head bowed, and he whispered, "Yes, those will do."

"Today is August the seventh in the year of our Lord 1894," Watson interjected.

"I was stabbed on the thirty-first of July. I remember the date because it was our anniversary. And, by the way, the love of my life is the one who killed me."

Holmes' eyebrows rose, but other than that, he was unruffled. "She never got over your rejection, and her pride grew as the years proved she couldn't entice you away from your first love, her twin sister. I go on to say that you were deceived at your wedding like the proverbial Leah and Rachel, yet you registered no complaint nor were coerced into staying silent."

A hint of red raced across Adam Blund's pasty face. His mouth opened but he remained speechless. John Watson did not have that problem. He blurted, "Seriously, Holmes, how could you possibly know that? Twin sisters? Jealousy? All by observing this man and without a family history being taken? How?"

Looking around the room, Holmes saw that all three of his companions leaned in, attentive. He smiled, slipped into his professorial mode, and pointed toward the ghost on the couch. "Observe, if you will, Adam wears no wedding ring, yet there is a pale marker on his ring finger indicating he has. Note also that several times since his arrival his hand has drifted toward his pocket watch, and on one occasion, he took it out to note the time and gently rubbed it, instinctively indicating it held a great affection for him. It was an easy deduction to surmise that whoever killed him also relieved him of his wedding ring; therefore, either a thief or an angry spouse. Since the pocket watch was not stolen, it follows that it was an angry spouse. Also note that although his clothes are expensive, they have been repaired; note the stitching of his cape around his right elbow, and on the inside of the seam on his right trouser leg. Two different types of stitches, therefore two different seamstresses. The stitching on the cape is haphazard, quickly sewn, only enough to get by, whereas the stitching on the trouser leg has been given careful attention to detail and is excellent work. The assumption I make is that the person who stitched his trousers cared very much for him, and I would be willing to gamble also gave him the pocket watch."

Adam Blund shook his head in awe. "Absolutely amazing! You are a genius, sir, seeing what others cannot and concluding trails like a hound upon the scent!"

Watson was not as easily awed. His eyes narrowed and he asked, "But the bit about twin sisters and being deceived into marrying the wrong one? How did you surmise that, Holmes?"

Holmes smirked as he sat back in his easy chair and took a long draw on his pipe. "Elementary, my dear friend. I read it in *The Times*. Three years ago, in the events section, an article was written by an infamous gossip about the Kyteler-Blund wedding and the rumor that the bride had been switched at the last moment. She remained hidden under the veil until the matrimony was announced, and the wedding meant for Beatrice Kyteler became the nuptials of Alice Kyteler."

Jonnie Alparts groaned, "That is horrible! Why didn't you say something, Mr. Blund? Why didn't Beatrice protest long and loud? You should have run to the magistrate and had the wedding annulled immediately."

Blund's eyes got a faraway cast. He sighed deeply and answered, "I was a coward, Mrs. Alparts, a horrible coward. When I lifted the veil, I was shocked. I had been told that Alice had suddenly taken ill and was not able to attend. The sisters are twins, but those of us who know them can tell them apart. I was mortified. I stepped back and was about to shout when Alice whispered, 'If you tell, Beatrice will die!' What really happened was not that Alice was ill, but Beatrice had been kidnapped and locked away until a week after the wedding. Then Alice sat both Beatrice and me down and told us the deed was done. There was nothing we could do about it, and if we tried, she would kill us both."

"And she has the resources to do it," Watson added. "The Kyteler family is old money and lots of it. They have been shipping magnates for two centuries. Legend has it the first Kyteler sold his soul to the devil and he has prospered them ever since."

"A distinct possibility," Holmes murmured as he took another draw on his pipe.

Francis crossed his huge arms and stared at Adam Blund. Something hadn't sat right with him. "Witches, wealth, and murder. Ghosts and broken hearts. Where do you start untangling this Gordian knot?"

Holmes tilted forward in his chair and asked another question. "Mr. Blund, do you recall anyone else being present when Beatrice Kyteler stabbed you? Where did it happen? Did she have help?"

"My memories are fleeting. I do remember that we were in our home. Her father had been visiting. I was escorting him to the door when suddenly I was hit from behind. I fell and then felt a sharp, awful pain in my chest. That is all I remember."

"Ah, so the father was a part of the murder?"

"I am not sure. Time is hard to judge, but it is possible," Blund agreed.

"Then that is where the investigation must start. With an investigation of the father." Holmes started to relight his pipe, satisfied he had a direction to pursue, when Watson interrupted him.

"I am afraid that won't be possible, Holmes." He handed the latest edition of *The Times* to his friend and pointed to a headline. It was an obituary notice. Andrew Kyteler had died of a massive stroke the previous day. Funeral arrangements were to be posted as soon as the family notified *The Times*.

Jonnie snorted, "That is damned convenient." Francis cringed at his wife's curse. "I'm sorry, husband; sometimes the old nature shows its ugly head." He nodded, understanding, and she continued, "The accomplice, who is also a witness, has been removed. Now what do we do?"

Holmes stared at the ceiling and the low clouds of pipe smoke that had risen to their common perch above his head. He looked back at Jonnie. "Why, we attend a funeral, my dear. We simply attend a funeral." He turned to Francis. "Francis, as far as we know, Mr. Blund's body has not yet washed up on any shore. I need you to ensure it doesn't. The fact that Adam can manifest here gives me reason to believe his body hasn't been recovered. As far as anyone knows, he has just disappeared or gone on a business trip. Mr. Blund, do you have any reason to believe that is not the case?"

"No, sir, I do not. I think," he paused as the weight of his next words settled on his heart, "I think that I am... or at least my body is still chained to an anchor lying on the bottom of the Thames."

"Very well then, sir. I don't know where you intend to lodge or even if you need to. But the rest of us have no recourse but to wait until the funeral before we can confront the woman involved."

Adam Blund nodded and then slowly, like fog beneath a morning sun, disappeared.

Holmes looked around the room. Everyone still gaped at the empty place the man had occupied, everyone except Francis, who was leaning against the wall and gently rubbing his chin. "Thoughts, Francis?" Holmes asked.

"Not much of one, sir, just a faint whisper, a voice in the back of my head that I can't quite hear. Might even be a scripture, sir. But right now, it's just out of reach. If I had to guess, I would think there is something off besides a ghost here, sir, but I can't put my finger on it."

A dry grin tried to find a place on Holmes' face but was not allowed entry; instead, he just looked back and slowly nodded.

******

In the basement of the Kyteler mansion, a tall young woman, her dark-brown hair drawn up in a bun and tucked in with pins, was dressed in a chemical worker's leather apron. She wore vulcanized gloves that came up to her elbows, and she breathed through a rubber and metal hood. A metal canister was attached to the bottom of the leather hood. The canister held a filter made from glycerin-soaked cotton and charcoal. Her grey eyes narrowed as she diligently studied her handiwork through the two large glass eyepieces centered in the hood. She dipped a paintbrush into a beaker full of boiling liquid, then carefully coated a bottle of wine with a thin layer of the extremely toxic chemical. After ensuring that every inch of the expensive bottle was covered, she placed it on a wine rack beneath the open awning window. "One down, one to go!" She laughed, then thought, *Oh, won't sister be surprised.*

The young woman failed to notice, because she did not know the peephole existed behind the faded painting of her grandfather, that someone was watching...someone with eyes exactly like hers.

******

As Holmes' entourage approached the Kyteler family mansion, they saw several buggies and assorted carriages, some carrying the black mourner's ribbon of a funeral procession, lined up along the street. The cab squealed to a halt, and Francis got out first and then assisted his lovely wife, who, as soon as her feet touched the ground, blurted from behind a dark mourner's veil, "Are you really sure this is necessary, Mr. Holmes?" She was dressed in black from head to foot; even her hat, and the feather jutting out of it, was black. It was an August afternoon, the hottest part of the day in muggy England. Holmes had insisted she accompany them to the funeral and dress the part of a grieving relative. He realized no one would know them but also trusted that no one would admit to not knowing them, just in case they were relatives who had been overlooked in the funeral announcements.

"Why do I have to be here?" she half shouted when she thought no one was listening.

Holmes frowned and cupped his hand over his mouth to answer. "Because, my dear, you are the best among us for discerning another's thoughts. And I expect we will need your gifts before this day is over."

She harrumphed and pointed back at her tall husband. "Francis is very adept at discerning both motive and intent.

You did not have to bring me along draped in hot black, sweltering in this heat, in the middle of a muggy day."

Watson laughed but felt her glower before he saw it and fell back on his overused excuse of coughing to try to hide it.

No one believed him, but Francis, skilled and greatly experienced at dealing with his wife, having the scars to prove it, dissuaded her from violence by intervening on everyone's behalf. "Jonnie, look at us. I'm seven feet tall, Holmes' face has been in the papers and is famous, and Watson has more friends than a store-bought politician. We need a distraction, every eye on someone besides us. And you, my beautiful wife, are more than proficient at providing distraction."

"Hmmph! Not much I can say to that." She planted her hands on her hips, looked up at her husband, and rolled her eyes. "You are a deceitful and cunning man." Her eyes laughed with the pleasure of her husband's compliment. She reached out to hug him and added, "But you are so good at it."

All three of her male companions sighed, and Watson prodded, "Can we proceed now?"

His remark was met by Jonnie's frown, but her husband placed both hands on her shoulders, turned her toward the front door, and pushed. Had Watson and Holmes not been there, he would have slapped her bountiful rear, but he refrained lest he hear about it later for hours.

The door opened, and a butler dressed in black inspected them. He didn't bat an eye but simply said, "This way, sirs and madam," then proceeded to escort them to a huge hall where a large crowd of mourners had already gathered.

Holmes surveyed the great hall. His attention was immediately drawn to the casket at the end of the room. A group of people stood around the casket staring down on Andrew Kyteler. Holmes spied Beatrice Kyteler, her eyes red and swollen. Next to her was her sister, Alice, almost an exact replica down to the same hair and figure. Alice wore a dress that was a mirror image of her sister's, only it was dark as her sister's was light. She leaned into her sister, her arm around Beatrice's shoulders. Alice's other arm hooked around a young woman with short black hair who wore a servant's uniform but was allowed the intimacy of the moment and apparently considered family.

Holmes' eyes scoured the family, noticing the way they moved, their posture, and even where they placed their hands. Then he blinked, shook his head, and blinked again. Adam Blund stood behind the servant girl, his hands resting on her shoulders. One of her hands responded to his gentle touch and was interlaced with his invisible fingers.

Francis, Jonnie, and Watson also studied the hall. Jonnie was the first to whisper, "No one here is mourning. I sense curiosity and layers of... of..."

"Devious calculation?" her husband offered.

"It's a room filled with treachery, for certain," Watson murmured.

She agreed, then added, "And witchcraft. The room reeks of witchcraft!" Her whisper carried intensity like a dark cloud bore thunder.

Holmes listened to his associates, but his eyes never left the party huddled around the casket. He saw Alice gently urge her sister to move away from the casket. As they moved, Holmes almost jumped. Andrew Kyteler's shadowy image was sitting up in his casket glaring at Alice. The ghost struck her, his hand passing through her body. The young woman's only response was to pull the shawl that draped her shoulders tighter.

Francis, also privy to the scene, turned his head toward Holmes. "Are you seeing what I am seeing?"

"If by that you mean the spectral antics of not one but two apparitions hovering around the most recently departed," he looked Francis in the eye, "I am indeed, sir. I am indeed."

Francis continued, "Mr. Holmes, something has been bothering me from the moment Mr. Blund mentioned that he was under a curse. I couldn't quite place it before, but now, seeing his hands upon the servant girl, I am really beginning to wonder. Please correct me if I'm misquoting from the Good Book, but isn't there a passage embedded somewhere in the book of the Wisdom of Solomon that says something like an undeserved curse..."

"'As the bird by wandering, as the swallow by flying, so the curse causeless shall not come.' Proverbs 28:2."

With a twinkle in his eye, Francis grinned and said, "My next guess, sir."

Holmes chuckled. "And while we are quoting from the proverbs, Francis, I cannot help but be reminded of another adage. 'If someone curses their father or mother, their lamp will be snuffed out in pitch darkness.'"

"Indeed, sir, and that may well be very applicable to this house."

******

Marie Armont, the petite French maid and former mistress of Adam Blund, knew immediately when the ghost of her former lover hovered behind her and laid his hands on her shoulders. She responded by reaching back. No one noticed because everyone near her was staring at the casket where Andrew Kyteler's body lay. She wondered how they would react if they, like she, could see into the spirit world and watch the frustrated ghost of Mr. Kyteler strike out at them. She did notice Alice draw her shawl a little tighter across her shoulders as she guided her murdering sister, Beatrice, to a quiet corner of the great hall.

As Marie stroked the spectral hand of her former lover, the hair on the back of her neck rose. She stopped before her body language gave away that she knew she was being watched. She took one last look at the pale figure in the coffin and the angry spirit that now sat on the casket, his legs dangling. Slowly, naturally, she drew her hand to her face, pretending to wipe her eyes. In so doing, she scanned the room and identified the man staring at her, a lanky man with a beak-like nose wearing a deerstalker cap. Their eyes met. He tipped his hat. She nodded back. She knew him. The chill that had warned her of his presence increased, causing goose pimples to rise across her body. She shivered, then forced a smile in his direction.

******

Alice Kyteler guided her grieving sister through the throng of mourners gathered in the great hall. The funeral guests, seeing Beatrice's red face and hearing her groans, parted like water beneath the prow of a ship to let her pass. Once the sisters entered the kitchen, Beatrice leaned against the countertop and turned off her weeping as quickly as a faucet. Not a single tear remained.

Alice's eyebrows rose and she sighed. "Would you like a glass of wine?"

Beatrice faked a sniffle and answered, "That would be nice."

Looking around the room, Alice located the wine bottle she had been searching for and grabbed it with her gloved hands. She reached into a drawer for the winged corkscrew and twisted it into the cork. Pressing down on the levers that stuck out from the cork, she pretended to strain and then handed the bottle to her sister. "I don't have enough hand strength. Would you give it a try?"

As she reached for the bottle, Beatrice's eyes widened and she jerked her hand back as if she had been offered a serpent. She tried to cover her reaction but saw her sister's stare and knew she was found out. Pushing through her blunder, she said, "Perhaps if you were to take your gloves off and get a good grip on the bottle, you could manage it, sister."

Alice glared back; her eyes cold like old tombstones on a winter day. Finally, she said, "How did you know?"

Beatrice's eyebrow rose. She stepped back, reaching for one of the large knives the cook had left on the countertop. "I saw you stirring up your little potion in the basement. Really, dear, don't you remember the peephole behind Grandfather's musty old portrait?"

Alice gritted her teeth, grabbed the neck of the wine bottle, and stepped toward her sister. "It only takes a touch. Just the mildest caress, as tender as a baby's cheek, will make your skin bubble, and after a moment it drips off your bones, working its agonizing way through your bloodstream. Your blood turns to acid, and finally your screams are cut short as your vocal cords melt."

Beatrice drew the knife and held it above her head, ready to bury it into her sister's chest. "You may get me, Alice, but I swear on all that is unholy, this knife will end you as well."

They paused at the brink of destruction, neither willing to cross over. Then, hearing the kitchen door open and the servant girl walk in, they quickly lowered their weapons.

Marie Armont pretended not to have noticed their posturing. "I saw you come in and knew you were distraught, so I went to your father's study and brought you something to ease your nerves." She held a silver platter with two glasses filled with dark golden-amber liquid. Raising it, she offered the refreshment to the women. "Perhaps this will help. Two small glasses of the good queen's favorite Islay single malt scotch."

Breathing a sigh of relief, Alice glanced at her sister and grabbed a glass. Beatrice also took a glass, neither noticing the gleam in Marie's eye as she watched them down the whiskey. She mimicked a common accent and said, "There now, that ought to cure what ails ya." Then she smiled, bowed her head respectfully, and walked out.

Alice looked back at her sister and frowned. She made no move to reach for the wine bottle. Beatrice countered with a question. "Why'd you steal him from me, Alice? I loved him so much!"

Alice tilted her head back. "Of course you did, and you could tell it by the way you and Father stabbed him and threw him into the Thames." Alice's laugh was hollow. Now that she actually spoke with her sister, she remembered there was a time when she loved her. She took another shot of the whiskey and continued, "Beatrice, Adam knew about the switch before it happened. He agreed to it because he knew that I would inherit more of Father's money. He did love you, dear, but he loved money more. And to be honest, while we are at it, I think," she leaned conspiringly toward her sister, "I think Marie put him up to it!"

"No! No! He loved me!" Beatrice screeched, disregarding her sister's revelation. "And then you killed our own father. Our father! Alice, you poisoned him. Why?"

Alice laughed again. She grabbed her sister's hand, holding it tight. "Because Father helped you instead of taking my side. That is profoundly simple. Why else would I? Beatrice, we were fools. I thought I was in love with

Adam. He seduced me and lavished kind words upon me."
Alice swung the wine bottle against the kitchen countertop,
shattering it into a hundred tiny pieces. "And that is why I
agreed to go along with his idea to lock you away for a
week and switch at the wedding. He convinced me to act
the villain, but all the while, he was cavorting with Marie!
Adam didn't love you or me! I spied him sporting with that
little sprite who just walked in here. I confronted him with
it, and he denied it, but the lipstick was still on his collar!"

Beatrice's eyes dropped, and the butcher knife she
gripped fell to the floor. "I thought he loved me."

Alice reached for her sister, and they embraced. "He
wasn't good enough for you, love." Alice tried to comfort
her sister; Beatrice didn't respond. Alice stepped back and
searched her face. Beatrice was pale. Her eyes fixed on the
two whiskey glasses that Marie had just brought them.
Alice gasped with shocked recognition, the room began to
spin, and though she tried to scream, it was too late.

******

Holmes watched as Marie left the funeral hall. He also
noticed when she slipped back in with a silver tray and two
whiskey glasses and made her way through the same doors
that the sisters had entered a few minutes before.

This should be interesting, he thought. A moment later,
she walked back into the great hall minus the silver tray and
began to mingle with the guests. Holmes approached her,
escorted at a discreet but protective distance by the
Alpartses and Watson.

As Holmes drew close, he caught the Frenchwoman's
attention. She smiled, closed out her conversation with an
English matron, and joined him. Adam Blund stood beside
her.

"Mr. Holmes, I am surprised to see you here. I did not know you were a friend of Mr. Kyteler."

"I was not. I am here in a professional capacity."

"Really? You're investigating then?"

"Yes, and ironically enough, my investigation has led me to you." Holmes saw the figure of Adam Blund stiffen at the remark. He also noted that the Frenchwoman seemed aware of Adam's presence.

She asked, "That being the case, would you mind accompanying me to a place where we may speak privately?"

"Surely, madam, but for propriety's sake, I must insist on my associates joining me." He motioned to the Alpartses and to Watson.

Marie followed his eyes and paled. "Apparently your worldview has changed, detective. You're starting to understand. Are you not?"

"It seems there is more to heaven and earth, Marie, than was previously dreamt of in my philosophies."

"Why do you say that?"

"Do you really want to play this game? I know who you are, even if my friend Blund does not. My associates have informed me that they have met you before."

Jonnie Alparts had drawn closer. "Yes, we have. Don't you remember, little witch? It was twenty years after your first assassination, and you were working with Napoleon."

"How could I forget?" Marie bowed her head. "I must say your complexion has improved remarkably. You can barely see the stitch scars."

Jonnie's face reddened and her hands balled into fists, but much to her husband's surprise, she did not attempt to strike the woman.

"So you've met?" Holmes interrupted. "Well enough and good. What's your part in this? Surely you don't need the money. Why go to the trouble of the long game?"

"Follow me, please." She started from the hall and led them into the private library of Andrew Kyteler. "You're wondering if I seduced Adam Blund and convinced him to betray his betrothed?" She looked at the ghost who had followed them into the study, the knife still protruding from his chest. His cheeks were hollow and dark rings circled his pale eyes. She reached for him and her hands passed through his spectral frame. "I am truly sorry, Adam. You were a good man, and I ruined it for you. Nothing I could say or do would help you understand or make it better. I did not consider that the sisters would have been so devious or vicious, but I should have known, and that was my mistake. My mission was simply to get control of the estate."

Adam Blund tried to speak but nothing came forth. He was fading, leaving this world, and his speech had already preceded him.

Moving to the library door, Francis Alparts stuck his head outside and then motioned for his wife to check the room. Watson was about to ask them what they were doing when Holmes grabbed his arm and put his finger to his mouth, commanding him to silence.

After a moment's thorough search, Francis drew back into the circle of conversation and whispered, "As far as we can tell, there are no hidden doors or peepholes."

Watson frowned and grumbled, "What on earth are you talking about, man?"

Marie nodded her thanks to the giant man, noting that Holmes hadn't been surprised by the Alpartses' actions. Then she continued in a subdued tone, "Dr. Watson and you, Adam." She looked up at the ghost who seemed to have diminished even more in the short time they had been in the library. "The reason I refer to the devious and vicious nature of the Kyteler sisters is because they come from a family that has bred that nature and nurtured those characteristics for centuries, if not longer."

Holmes was nodding. Marie raised an eyebrow and kept talking. "Apparently, Mr. Holmes and Mr. and Mrs. Alparts know of which I speak. And sadly," she turned to the apparition that could now only watch, "Adam, you did not. You were the exception, the anomaly, if you will. I am not sure the sisters even knew, but I'm convinced your father-in-law did. He talks in his sleep."

Adam's eyes rolled and a tear stole down his pale cheek.

Jonnie Alparts' eyes narrowed, and she moved closer to her husband, placing an arm through his while gripping him possessively with her other hand.

Watson interrupted the awkward pause, "Two questions trouble me, madam. The first is how do you know such history? And second, what is your part in it?"

Holmes raised an eyebrow of agreement and waited for Armont's response.

Sighing, she turned to the whiskey decanter that sat on a side desk in the library. She found five small glasses and poured a two-finger shot in each. Jonnie Alparts' eyes were riveted on her. She saw Marie's eyes focus for just a moment on the golden liquid. Then, just as the Frenchwoman put the glass to her lips, Jonnie struck like a cobra, grabbing Marie's hand and hissing, "Not this time, witch! Dr. Watson, if you wish to live to see the top of the hour, I strongly suggest you put your shot glass back on the tray."

Watson, who loved his whiskey, held the small glass close to his lips but froze at Jonnie's warning. He eyed the liquid as if it was exactly the poison it was and slowly set it down.

Holmes said, "Thank you, Jonnie. I was a bit slow on that, but thankfully you were not." He turned back to Marie whose hand was held in Jonnie's viselike grip. "Now, if you would be so kind as to continue with your story."

"If you don't mind?" Marie jerked her hand away from Jonnie and placed the shot glass on the silver tray. "Well." She exhaled a long breath. "Believe it or not, I am also grateful. I can tell my masters that I was discovered before I could self-terminate. Considering who it is that discovered me, they will believe it." She must have been expecting the word *masters* to elicit a response from the people watching her, but seeing none, she shrugged and kept talking. "The Kytelers own the majority of the tugboats in England and many in Europe. Whoever controls the tugboats controls shipping. If a tug, for one reason or another, is not available to maneuver a large vessel into port, it doesn't come in."

Francis shook his head, cursing under his breath. "Brilliant. Lowest investment, highest return. A monopoly without a monopoly. Nothing since the East India Company's glory days has had the potential to control so much with so little."

A deceptive smile slipped across Marie Armont's beautiful face. "Convenient that, and also an interesting historical note that when said company was dissolved by an act of Parliament in 1874 and taken over by the government, the men who had previously owned it, and made their immense fortunes from it, still controlled its assets and its army."

Watson gasped, "Bloody thieves!" And then he smirked. "Shrewd and ruthless."

Marie stared at him and added, "And they are only one group led by just a few families, and those are just the families in Britain. When you consider the pacts and alliances the world over, with sects like those on every continent, then you begin to understand the term *Masters.*"

Sherlock Holmes took up where Marie left off. "And they control every vice from prostitution to opium, and every trade route, and have their hands in arms manufacturing and distilleries, and of course, religion and newspapers and education."

"My God!" Jonnie Alparts groaned. "How can this be? It's like a secret world government, an... an antichrist network."

Holmes nodded. "More like Antichrist's, Jonnie. And has been for a very long time."

Marie perched on the library's large overstuffed chair. "What are you going to do with me?"

Holmes sat on the couch across from her, took his pipe out of his pocket and a pinch of dark herb from his pouch, and lit it. His stare never left Marie Armont.

"We have two situations here, Miss Armont. We have the immediate: the deaths of Andrew Kyteler and Adam Blund and by now, I suppose, of Alice and Beatrice Kyteler as well."

The Frenchwoman shrugged slightly, and Holmes continued, "And we have the long game, the very, very long game." A puff of smoke curled around his head and quickly dissipated. "We must take them—"

A shout interrupted him, then another, and then loud screams, "Fire! Fire!"

Francis Alparts ran down the hall. Seconds later he returned. "Flames have started in the kitchen and are spreading throughout the house. I am sure it was deliberate. People are panicking, racing for the doors, trampling each other."

Holmes looked at the sturdy walls that surrounded the library. "There are no doors or windows to this room!"

Francis Alparts laughed and strode to the middle of the far wall. "Where would you like one?" He struck the wall with his fists, pounding them like a boxer would his foe. The plaster fell, then the wood frame, and finally he began to hammer through the brick that stood between them and freedom. A fist-sized hole appeared; bricks began to crumble. He kicked and a larger hole broke open as sparks and cinders started raining down on them. Francis grabbed Jonnie and shoved her through the hole. Watson was next.

Marie Armont hesitated. "They have me, Mr. Holmes. They know I entered this room with you. They have eyes everywhere. They set the fire, and even if their agents die in the blaze, it will be worth it to silence me. I am a dead woman."

Holmes looked at Francis and then cast a glance at Watson, who frantically motioned them to jump through the wall. "Swoon! Quickly! Act as though the poison worked. Fall over now!"

Francis, quick as ever, smirked, then picked up the limp body of the woman and stepped through the hole. Holmes was quick to follow him. They tramped across the rubble and then out into the garden. A large crowd of surviving mourners gathered, forming a wary circle around Holmes' entourage.

Watson bent low and grabbed Marie's hand to take her pulse. He looked at Holmes, shocked. "She's dead, man! How did that happen? I thought..." Holmes shushed him in mid-shout. One look at Holmes' face and Watson, long experienced with his friend's trickery, understood. Watson began again louder, "What a horrible waste! A beautiful woman overcome by smoke inhalation. She must have been asthmatic."

Holmes rolled his eyes at Watson's overdramatization. He was a great physician but would never acquire a role on the stage. Jonnie bent close to the good doctor, pinched his arm, and whispered, "Enough! Just shake your head and cover her face with this kerchief."

Watson reddened, then complied. Francis picked up the body, and they slowly walked through the crowd, all but one of whom now stood facing the inferno of the Kyteler mansion. Holmes did not see the dark face turned aside to watch him leave.

Two hours later

Watson had almost finished applying carbolic acid to the wounds on Francis' hands and wrapping his sausage-like fingers with gauze. Francis shook his head at his friend and said, "My good doctor, Watson, you know this is most unnecessary. My wounds heal quickly, and these"—he laughed as he raised his bandaged hands— "make me look like a recently wrapped Egyptian mummy!" His chuckling came to an abrupt stop like a blind man slamming into a brick wall. His beautiful wife's eyebrows were lining her hairline in a fashion that Francis was acutely aware would cause him immeasurable grief if he did not immediately heed their delicate direction. He sighed, ceased his laughter, and backpedaled. "But I am grateful for your ministrations." He tried moving his fingers and frowned as he discovered the bandages were keeping them stiff.

Holmes entered the room after cleaning off the smut and ash and plaster dust of their recent adventure. When he saw Francis staring at his fingers, he burst out laughing. "Francis, you make Watson look like an ancient Egyptian mortician. If he had wrapped your head, you'd look just like the creature from Bram Stoker's novel *The Jewel of Seven*

Stars. Some type of revived mummy, I believe they called it."

Jonnie scowled and threw down the little socks she was knitting. "I think I will check to see if the witch has awakened." She stomped out of the very quiet room. As soon as the bedroom door shut behind her, Watson chuckled. Holmes joined him, desperately trying to subdue the noise of his laughter. Francis, having an even harder time, grabbed a pillow and stuffed his head in it. Then his laughter turned to stone as his eyes fixed on the knitting Jonnie had thrown down. Holmes observed the direction of his stare and Watson noticed a heartbeat later. She was knitting little socks; they were pink. This time Watson's laugh could not be contained. All the blood ran from Francis' large face, and he looked worse than if he had seen another ghost.

At that moment Jonnie walked back into the room holding Marie Armont by the waist. She eased the petite Frenchwoman to the couch and looked up to see Francis' face, then noticed the little pink socks in his large hands. He looked at her, a question etched in his face. She blushed, shook her head, and hurled herself into his arms.

Holmes sat back in his chair, and Watson moved the wicker rocker closer. It was a special moment and none of them were inclined to ruin it.

Finally, Jonnie took a deep breath and said, "All right then, I wasn't sure till just a moment ago." Holmes' head tilted, an unasked question upon his lips. "It was Marie. Other than being a witch, she is also a certified midwife."

Holmes glanced at Marie, who nodded and turned her gaze on Dr. Watson, whose celebration had turned to a frown.

"I will discuss my experience with you later, Dr. Watson, but I can assure you, it is more than herbs and potions. Of course, the antiseptic you just used on Francis is made from coal tar, and the pain relief was from a flower or the bark of a willow tree, but what do I know?"

Before Watson could respond, Holmes intercepted the conversation. "Moving right along, we need to talk. The fire removed evidence of both crime and the proof thereof, and apparently, even Mr. Blund has moved on."

"So much for the idea of a curse then," Francis murmured.

Marie turned toward him. "Curse?"

Francis answered, "Mr. Holmes and I thought we had discerned a curse in play, one Adam Blund had become entangled with because of his iniquity. We thought it might have been placed on him by Beatrice, or even Alice, and…" He tried to stroke his chin as he pondered but, realizing he couldn't because of the bandages wrapped around his fingers, blew out a disgusted harrumph and went on with his thought. "Maybe he was, and when Alice or Beatrice died and their bodies were burned in the fire, the curse was broken, allowing him to move on?"

Marie smiled sadly. "You are right, Francis Alparts. Adam was cursed, and with more than one curse. The family he fatally aligned himself with was independent of the Masters, but they had their own affiliations. They were a wicked and old line whose ancestors warred with the Christian missionaries who had crossed over from what was then called Gaul around the fourth century. They were shamans, involved with demons and spells, empowered by innocent blood."

Jonnie, who had started to warm toward Marie, stiffened and in a cold tone asked, "Is that how they found you? I mean, you are a witch, are you not?"

Marie sighed and looked at her hands. "I think that word "witch" may be a bit broad. It is typically applied to any woman who has spiritual gifts. I have gifts, but I do not bow to the old gods. I hate those creatures. At the same time, I have found myself an outcast by the cultural religion of this age. To be honest, I am a lot of things, some of which you are aware. In my servitude to the Masters, I have committed adultery, I have murdered, I have stolen, I have borne false witness, but one thing I have not done and will never do is: I have not bowed my knee nor worshiped the idols of the Masters. I have not, and I will not. But I tell you something else." Her eyes glistened as she stared unflinchingly at Sherlock Holmes. "Adam Blund had bowed, and the curse that held him was not because of some paltry spell a jealous woman had bound on him. It was for another reason. Moses wrote in his books, 'Cursed is the one who makes a carved or molded image, an abomination to the Lord, the work of the hands of the craftsman, and sets it up in secret.' Adam Blund and the Kytelers and the Master families are all idol worshipers. What's more, they know I escaped, Mr. Holmes. I sense it deeply, and they will be coming for me. They are coming..."

Idol Hands

Holmes wondered if he would have to rent a larger flat. Bob was learning to walk and inevitably knocked over whatever his small fingers could grasp to pull up his little body. His mother, being a new mother who had waited a hundred years for a child, hovered like a flustered shadow. Watson's lips had learned better than to part, but his eyes did not have a problem flaunting his amusement as Jonnie constantly pleaded and then nagged and finally surrendered to the brilliant young man's hardening will. It also amused Watson, who stayed a long way from the fray, that when the little boy's father lumbered into the room, with his quick hand that had no problem finding its way to the round bottom of the rebellious infant, the child's behavior changed. He still laughed and played and climbed over his father's large frame to land in his lap, cuddle up, and take a nap, but he did it with a lot less childish mischief, which antagonized his beautiful mother all the more.

Holmes' musings were brought to a stop with a loud clamor at the front door. Mrs. Hudson was railing against a street urchin, and the whole house was privy, whether it chose to be or not, to the conversation.

Holmes stuck his head out the apartment door and looked down the stairs. Mrs. Hudson held a young boy, probably nine or ten years old, at bay with her broom. The young man wore old but not filthy clothes; one of his shoes had a hole in the top and the other didn't match.

"Yer canna go up, lad. He is resten wiv the Alpartses and Watson, and I'm sure that 'e doesn't know ya or want ta see ya."

"But ma'am, I 'ave instructions ter deliver a message from 'is bruvver."

"Child, that's wot they all say. Right, I'm sure yer wouldn't know 'is bruvver if 'e stood beside yer."

Holmes sauntered out of the apartment and, looking down from the top of the stairs, interrupted the conversation. "Mrs. Hudson! I know the boy; he works for me on occasion. It's fine. Just allow him to come up, please."

The young man beamed and sped to the top of the stairs. Holmes chuckled as the ragamuffin raced away from the gatekeeper.

Holmes stooped to greet the young man. "How are yer, Robbie, then, eh, mate? Yer doin' well, right, how's yor mum?"

The boy's eyes brightened; then his voice took a scolding tone. "Mr. Holmes, you don't have to talk like an uneducated street person to me. You're a gentleman and I have been learning my spelling and words and such as you told me, so when I grow up, I can be a gentleman as well. My mother is better, thanks to Dr. Watson. He has been seeing her regularly."

Surprise and approval danced in Holmes' eyes. "Robbie, that is wonderful. Now come in; I want you to meet some special people." He opened the apartment door and the little boy walked through. Holmes then turned back to Mrs.

Hudson, who stood at the bottom of the stairwell. "Thank you, Mrs. Hudson, for watching out for us. But Robbie works for me, and he is a good boy. Now would you be so gracious as to fix him a hearty breakfast and, if you would"—he cupped his hands about his mouth and whispered—"make enough for him to take home to his mother."

Mrs. Hudson smiled. She didn't mind the extra work and was glad Holmes cared for those who struggled to care for themselves. "Certainly, Mr. Holmes. I would be happy to."

When Robbie walked through the apartment door, he stopped frozen in his thin-soled tracks. Francis Alparts stood to his full height and stared down on the small boy. Watson tried to keep from smiling, and Jonnie threatened her huge husband with a *you better not frighten that poor child* look. So Francis was also frozen. Finally, he said, "Are you the famous Robbie Scott that Holmes and Dr. Watson are always talking about?"

The boy's eyes were wide, and his head tilted so far back to stare up at Francis that he almost fell over. He gulped and slowly nodded. Then his eyebrow cocked and his respiration evened out. Stepping back, he took a quick glance around and saw Watson trying not to laugh, and that did it for him. He slipped into his street vernacular and asked, "I do not know about the famous part, sir, but yes, me name is Robbie Scott, right. And 'oo might yer be, sir?"

Francis grinned and stooped down to where he didn't loom quite so much over the child. "My name is Francis Alparts, Robbie, and this is my lovely wife, Jonnie Alparts, and my little boy, Bob."

Robbie blinked at Jonnie, rubbed his eyes, and blinked again. Then he looked back at Francis. "Noooo... yor teasin' me, sir. A lady that beautiful cannot be married ter you."

Jonnie's scowl at Francis turned to beaming. Her husband straightened, crossed his arms, and made a mean face, deliberately looming over the boy, who was extremely streetwise and had him figured out. Francis might look like a monster, but Robbie knew he had a soft heart, so he immediately started working on Jonnie. "Yor not gonna let this big man 'urt me, are yer, m'lady?" he said in a trembling little voice.

Holmes had walked in on the last part of the conversation. His eyes narrowed and an overdone frown accompanied them. "Robbie! Leave the Alpartses alone! They are nice people, and you are not to take advantage of them, do you hear me?"

The boy bowed his head, mostly to hide his grin, but he looked humble enough to bring Jonnie to his aid.

"Mr. Holmes, don't scold that poor boy; he can't help it if he thinks I am a beautiful lady and my husband a large bruiser!"

Robbie's head popped up, his eyes twinkling and his snaggle-toothed smile on display. "See there, Mr. Holmes, he can't help it..."

Holmes looked down his glasses and shook his head. "Robbie, Mrs. Hudson is fixing you a grand breakfast, and she is making enough for you to take home to your mother."

"Thank you, Mr. Holmes. You have always taken care of me and my mother, and I am extremely grateful," he answered in a form of the Queen's English that would make a grammarian proud.

Holmes pulled out a pound note and said, "You are important to me, Robbie. Make sure this gets to your mother."

A tear rolled down the boy's cheek as he took the money and stuffed it into his coat pocket. "I will, Mr.

Holmes, I will." He started to turn away but looked at Holmes and hugged him tightly around his long legs. Holmes bent low and returned the embrace. Watson stared, wide-eyed. He had never seen Holmes embrace anyone. After a moment the boy broke the hug, wiped his nose on his sleeve, and said, "Here is the note from your brother." He placed a small crumpled piece of paper in Holmes' outstretched hand and then ran out the door and down the stairs yelling for Mrs. Hudson.

Holmes unfolded the paper and stared at it. He started to gape, and then as full understanding came, his face turned ashen. Francis reached for him, thinking he might pass out. Holmes handed him the paper and dropped into his overstuffed chair. There were no words on the sheet, just a hastily sketched drawing of a woman's face screaming.

"It's a banshee," he whispered. "Mycroft sent me a sketch of a banshee."

Everyone was confused. Watson stared at his friend, amazed that in the space of five minutes he had seen Holmes do not one but two things he had never seen him do before: hug a young street urchin and get struck dumb. "What is it, Holmes? What's wrong?"

Holmes stared back at Watson but didn't see him. His eyes were focused on an old memory of him and his brother, to the time when they had been discussing the worst-case scenarios a nation could experience and how they would notify one another if either one ever got word that a horrible disaster had come upon the country. They had finally settled on a simple pictorial code, with different pictures meaning different things. The screaming banshee was the worst of the worst; it meant disaster imminent, situation out of control, personal death expected soon. And Mycroft had just sent it to him.

Holmes inhaled deeply and took the whiskey that Watson handed him. His friends were deathly quiet. Finally, Holmes shivered, shook himself, and looked up at them. "Trouble is coming, probably war. Mycroft's life is in danger, and perhaps our own. I am certain we are being watched. We have a meeting place but it may be compromised. So here is what we need to do."

******

Marie Armont was extremely uncomfortable. She did not like crowds and was surrounded by at least ten thousand people in the Surrey Gardens Music Hall. It would have been tolerable, she could have toughed it out, if they had been gathered to hear an orchestra or watch a play, but no... These fools—commoners and aristocrats, cobblers and cabbies, physicians and soldiers, housemaids and even women who plied an ageless trade—were gathered to hear a Baptist preacher! It was almost more than she could stomach. Had her duties not bound her, she would have run to the nearest exit and searched for the closest pub. But she had trailed an agent here, a man she had been watching for days. He must have known she followed him because he had taken a half-dozen turns, backtracked, and disappeared a number of times, only to have her gifts point her back to his trail every time. Now he was here. She had seen him enter the hall, pretending to be a seeker. He had even taken a hymnal and a fan and was now seated three rows ahead in the large auditorium, waiting on the famous preacher Charles Spurgeon to walk to the podium.

Marie had done many things in the war against the families and never batted an eye. She had slain and stolen and slept with her enemies, but she had never gone to church with them. Her skin felt clammy; her heart was pounding. Most witches did not go to worship meetings, and she knew it. She didn't know how to act or what would occur. She knew about spiritual things and was gifted in their use. She knew Protestant Christianity had no place for the psychically gifted and labeled them witches, and, had English law permitted, would have taken any they found and hanged and burned them. She was extremely uncomfortable to say the least, but also curious. Her mission was to track the agent to his source, and her journey had led her here.

Suddenly her thoughts shattered. Every intuitive sense she owned screamed out that something terrible was about to happen. Her muscles tightened; the air became heavy, causing her skin to itch. Chills raced through her body in waves, but she was the only one who could feel it. Her eyes riveted on the back of the man she had followed into the hall. He stood up from his seat in the pews, looked to the balcony, then to his right, and nodded. Then he politely excused himself as he walked the length of the aisle he had been seated in.

When he reached the end of it and came almost to the exit door, a terrified scream of "Fire! Fire!" rang from both the balcony and the area the man had signaled. People jumped to their feet and began racing down the aisle. They had entered the building to deal with their animalistic nature; now they proved why they needed to be there. At first people tried to be orderly. Then someone panicked, then others, and then those being pushed shoved back, with everyone pressing toward the small exits. No doors were labeled, and no one was sure where to head. Fear ravaged the mass of endless people trapped and screaming. Shouts of anguish raked the ears that had expected hymns.

Smoke started to fill the building, adding to the confusion of the worshipers. The night was already hot and muggy, and the windows did not draw any breeze. People squeezed and pushed and fell. Marie saw an old woman go down, her frail husband desperately trying to pull her up. A large man stepped on her, then another, breaking her husband's hold on her hand and shoving him to the floor. A child left in a pew wailed, searching for his mother, who had fallen beneath the seats, crushed.

Marie watched in despair. She sensed the shouts of fire had been false, but the fear that drove the people, crushing the life from them in the horrible rush to reach the exits, was real. She stepped over the pew, reached for the wailing child, and held it to her, huddling over it, shielding it from the throng. A large woman with a red velvet traveling hat fell as she frantically tried to shove her way through the throng, causing those pushing against her to fall with her. The wave tumbled, slamming people against the wooden pews and the cement floor, and Marie and the child she shielded, and then everything went dark.

******

Holmes left a little after midnight, destination undisclosed. Watson wanted to go with him, but Holmes convinced him to dress in a long coat and a deerstalker hat and leave from the front door around 11:00, while Francis and he entered the attic and carefully stepped across a dozen connected ceilings till, dripping with sweat, they found their way into an abandoned factory building attached by the roof roadway.

Then they moved from ceiling to sewer and entered the London sewer system. After traveling for hours, they exited in the basement of a private school. They waited through the day and left in the darker hours of the next night. Francis was a wary creature and Holmes had a nose for being followed; neither one sensed that they were. Finally, after acquiring a covered cab that had been secreted away for just such a moment, they arrived around dawn of the second day at the Goodwood Derby track. Holmes drove the cab around back to the stalls and then had Francis follow him to a storage room in the back of the huge barn. The straw had been moved and the hidden door in the floor revealed. Francis tugged on it and the old board creaked. Holmes set one foot down into the gloom, his pistol drawn.

Francis grasped his shoulder and whispered, "A bullet might hit you, sir. It would hardly faze me; let me go first." Holmes nodded and stepped aside. The old stairs screeched a wooden complaint as the giant man slowly entered the gloom, Holmes close behind him.

"Mycroft!" Holmes whispered as loudly as he could. "Mycroft, it's Sherlock. Are you here, man?"

A groan answered him. "Sherlock, it's your voice, but who is that with you? He looks like he stepped out of Ringling Brothers."

A lantern lit, and Holmes and Francis saw the pale face of his brother, Mycroft, illuminated by it. Mycroft was an extremely fat man. His jowls had jowls. His large head rested on huge shoulders that seemed void of any semblance of a neck. But there was not a more brilliant man in Britain. Mycroft brought to British military intelligence what Sherlock Holmes did to Scotland Yard. He saw clues that others were blind to and correlated data into amazingly accurate conclusions. The two brothers were some of England's greatest treasures.

Sherlock's eyes took in his brother's haggard appearance, and he was shocked to see how his clothes hung on him. Mycroft had lost a great deal of weight. The dark circles under his eyes told Sherlock that it had not been easy for him the last few weeks.

Noticing his brother's face, Mycroft said, "Really, brother, is it that bad? You look like you've seen a ghost. Is my appearance so appalling that you can hardly look at me?"

Holmes scowled. "Mycroft, I have seen a ghost, and he looked much better than you. And he'd been dead a week and had a butcher's knife sticking out of his chest! But I must say I am dearly glad to see you, brother. Your note chilled me and now your tattered clothes and sickly features have added a dire frost to that same chill. What is going on? Hurry now and do not keep me waiting!"

Mycroft tried to laugh and wound up coughing. While he spasmed, Holmes drew closer and saw him in a better light. "Mycroft, you're bleeding, man! Have you been shot?"

"Not shot, Sherlock, stabbed, but I fared better than Eglon the Moabite. The blade did not pierce my belly as intended but only nicked it a bit. See, it pays to be a man of weight, dear brother, despite your spindly physician's constant reprimands. Had I not been able to bring a ton of flesh to my rescue and suffocate my would-be assailant beneath its folds, I wouldn't be here."

Francis cringed at the picture Mycroft painted and was glad the shadows hid his face.

Holmes just shook his head and answered, "Your encyclopedic biblical references may illustrate a point, but they will not serve you in the long run. But since you obviously have matters in hand and haven't bled to death in the meantime, I will not belabor the point. So back to it then. What is going on?"

"Gold, Sherlock, simple golden greed. Gold was discovered in the Witwatersrand area of the South African Republic. If the reports are true, then that area is about to become the destination for thousands of prospectors. The information I have implies the find mimics the California Gold Rush of 1849. Possibly a quarter of the world's gold is now available for whoever can stake a claim first."

"Mycroft, I fail to understand why a gold rush in South Africa causes a national calamity in London. You know as well as I that the large majority of those seekers will come home empty-handed, if they come home at all and are not buried in unmarked graves somewhere in the African soil."

"You are correct, of course, my little brother. However, you fail to see the long game. This is not about the gold that can be dug out of the earth, but about the groundswell that surrounds it, the merchants and transportation owners and investors, and the large migration of people that will stimulate global trade and colonization and...revolt. And it is the latter that has brought me to a basement beneath a barn reeking of horse shit and encrusted blood. And booger it, to top this folly off, I am sure I was followed." Mycroft hobbled out of the shadows, shoved his massive belly past his brother, and held the lantern up to Francis. He gasped. "So, you do keep strange companions, dear brother. I had heard reports, but this is enlightening." He scratched one of his jowls, covered in a four-day-old beard, and murmured, "And this might be the best of times to have him. Are the reports true? Does he have the strength of ten men and is he impervious to bullets?"

"The last time I measured, sir, I had diminished a bit in strength and now only have the strength of seven men, which is approximately two English tons. As to bullets, my skin can resist all but point-blank rifle range, and even then, it needs to be a very powerful rifle," Francis explained.

Holmes, who had never thought to ask, blinked at his friend. "Really, Francis. My goodness, man! I never realized."

Francis reddened and shrugged his massive shoulders.

"See there, Sherlock. I told you mass had its benefits," Mycroft chided, then continued his lecture. "The Boers want independence. And this influx of humanity is going to bring the wealth and the arms to make a play for it. And behind it all is the diamond trade; Cecil Randolph controls, literally controls, the diamond markets of the world. He tells Vicky to jump and she hikes her skirts and skips. But truth be known, and few there be that know it, that in spite of all Randolph's posturing and public support of the empire, he wants his own nation. Even has a name for it, I hear—Randesia or some sort of tripe like that."

Holmes' mind was racing literally around the world. Finally, he came to a screeching halt, looked at Francis, who was jogging alongside him, and whispered, "Masters?"

Mycroft's reaction was immediate. "Did you say Masters?! Sherlock, how did you hear of the families? But I should have known that it was a sorry miscalculation and underestimation of your deductive abilities. Of course you would know. But how you came to it, now that's a mystery. Eh?"

The question in Mycroft's voice caused Holmes to pause. "Mycroft, an answer for an answer. I will tell you how I know if you divulge your part in the long game. Now, brother, the shoe is on the other foot."

Stepping back, Mycroft leaned against the basement wall, looking like a deflated walrus. His eyes focused on a vision only he could see. Then he shook his massive frame and answered, "Our father served them, Sherlock. And like so many others the secret eventually killed him. But before he died, he shared the burden. We are all in the game; most live and die and never know. But a few, a very few I might add, either by gaining great wealth or political power or superior skill desired by the families, are brought behind the curtain. To the real history of the world. The real powers, the families, known by their servants as the Masters. Great steps are taken to ensure their secrets; nations have fallen and wars been lost to preserve their mastery and their identity. But then something unexpected happens, like the discovery of gold in South Africa, and suddenly the balance is undone, and measures are taken to restore it or form a new cabal. Every continent has its own behind-the-scenes Masters. Some continents have more than one, depending on the wealth and population of that arena."

Mycroft scratched his four-day beard and sat down on a large square bale, took a breath, and continued. "I am a pawn, as are you, in the great game, only I know I am and you have just discovered your place. With the discovery of gold and the transfer of great wealth, a new family has risen and invaded the arena. It is aware of the others and has attacked and mauled a few. This new group is selfish and unwilling to share the planet. And it is led by Cecil Randolph."

Francis abruptly shuddered and sniffed deeply. "We have a problem. A fire has been started in the barn above us. I can smell the acrid scent of petrol distillates used to start it. We need to make our way out of here."

Holmes moved toward his brother to help him mount the stairs and was thrust off the first step by Francis, who had opened the hidden hatchway to the basement. Francis jumped back, coughing. "It's right over us and raging. We can't get out that way!"

******

Marie Armont awoke with a pounding head and a bruised body. The child she had tried to protect was nowhere in sight. After her eyes focused and she was able to sit up, she discovered she wasn't where she had expected to be. She was not on a spit over a fire in hell or, worse yet, in an English hospital surrounded by infection and calloused nurses. Instead, she sat on a large dark leather sofa with a crocheted blanket spread over her. Light came through a large window at the end of the sofa, and through the window she could hear the jingle of horse reins and the clip-clop of their hooves as they met the cobblestone streets. There was also the incessant music of one of William Booth's terrible but well-intentioned brass bands.

As she looked around the room, she saw that it was a library filled with a huge assortment of books. A couple of overstuffed chairs and a simple wicker rocker stood next to a fireplace, thankfully unlit in the middle of summer. Someone cleared their throat and instantly she turned in their direction. Leaning over a desk with his hands under his bearded chin sat a tall man of solid build. He had piercing eyes but a kind face. When he realized Marie was awake, he walked from behind his desk and sat across from her in an overstuffed chair. Marie's eyes never left him. Crossing his legs, he leaned back, steepled his long fingers, and continued looking at her. He was an extremely lean, rugged man with a faint scar that ran from above his right eye and down his hairline. *A soldier perhaps,* she thought.

He simply stared at her, alternating between thoughtfulness and frustration, before he finally opened his mouth and asked in a kindly curious tone, "What are you?"

That was not what she had been expecting. She folded her arms and raised her eyebrows but didn't answer immediately. Then slowly, carefully feeling her way through whatever traps might be placed in her path, she replied, "The fact you ask such a question assumes you have an answer in mind; you didn't ask me who I was but what I was. To be honest, no one upon first meeting me has ever asked me that." Her French accent, blunted by forty years in England, crept through enough to give her speech a husky sound more like a purr than the high-pitched nasal twang so often heard on London's streets. "So, who… or, to honor your specific question, *what* do you think I am?"

The man's penetrating gaze probed her features, and crow's feet framed the faintest twinkle in his eyes. She could tell he was not a cruel man, and yet she knew him to be a warrior, but of what army she was not sure.

"I think you have been mislabeled. I know that you have referred to yourself as a witch on several occasions and that you look like you are in your mid- to late twenties, but reports of you first appeared in France almost one hundred years ago. So, I am in a quandary. You don't bear the stain of demonic connivance and yet you clearly manifest some type of mystical powers. You have worked for the French and for," he leaned in closer and his speech quieted, "the Masters, so to answer your question, I do not know what you are; I just know what I see, and I am puzzled." He cocked his head, returning her gaze and her question.

She rolled her shoulders, trying to ease the tension gripping her neck. Before she woke in this man's library, she would have had simple answers to his question. But now… since he had reframed her whole life in a single paragraph, clarity was turning to confusion. Of course she was a witch. Witches cast spells and manipulated; they saw things on people, and they saw into realms most people didn't even know existed. But—she paused, ancient bells ringing in her mind—this man in a matter of moments had stripped her of her identity and left her speechless, not because she had no words but because she had no answer.

A diminutive tremor of her lips told him she was off balance. He absentmindedly traced his fingers across the scar that framed his face. He wanted to be kind, but dark experience earned with blood told him it was better to push hard than let them push you and bleed for it.

He continued, "You were not responsible for the panic last night; you went so far as to be trampled underfoot in order to save a child. We found you huddled over the child. He is all right, by the way."

Marie breathed a sigh of relief she knew wouldn't go unnoticed by her interrogator.

"So, Marie, why were you at Surrey Gardens Music Hall last night? I am confident it was not to hear my father preach."

Marie responded to that revelation with a tilted head and raised eyebrow.

"My name is Thomas Spurgeon, by the way." He leaned toward her, his hand extended. "And it is good to meet you."

She cautiously took his large, callused hand. When she touched him, a gentle current of energy ran through their hands. She jerked back. The only time she had ever felt that before was when she touched another practitioner.

This time it was Thomas Spurgeon's turn to raise an eyebrow. All he said was "Interesting…" He sat back in his chair and looked at her in a different light. "Apparently the Spirit knows His own."

"That is ridiculous!" she huffed, crossing her arms.

Thomas Spurgeon crossed his arms, reflecting her posture. "How do you explain what just happened?"

"Your religion has persecuted people like me for hundreds, if not thousands, of years. Your Old Testament even spells it out quite clearly: 'suffer not a witch to live.' And you tell me that you just got a revelation that flies in the face of the clear teachings of your ancient tome simply because one of us scuffed our feet across a rug and discharged static electricity?"

Spurgeon shook his head and chuckled. Her eyes narrowed and a dark scowl settled across her face. He continued to laugh, shaking his head more aggressively.

"What? What is it? Why are you laughing?"

"Marie." He pointed to the floor in the room. "There is no carpet."

******

Holmes pulled his wounded brother back from the stairs. Smoke started to drift down into the basement. He could see beads of sweat dripping off Francis' reddened face.

Mycroft said, "Sherlock, on the far wall, behind the shelves, is a hidden door. You can use it to escape."

Francis didn't need another admonition. He ripped into the shelves Mycroft had indicated and broke open the antique frame of an old door. Dust added to the smoke filling the room, and a dark corridor greeted them. Francis sniffed again. "Nothing in there except dirt and stone. I'll take the lead." He nodded toward Mycroft. "Unless you want me to help him while you scout the way for us."

Holmes was busy wrapping a piece of broken shelf with burlap from empty feed sacks tucked away in the basement. He dipped it into a barrel of horse liniment and struck a match, instantly rewarded with a makeshift torch. "If you don't mind, Francis, I will guide the way and you assist Mycroft."

Francis shook his head while Mycroft chuckled at Holmes' response and said, "Oh, yes, let the monster help the fat man."

"Really, Mycroft?" Holmes chided.

"Are you offended because I referred to your associate as a monster?"

Francis gently placed Mycroft's arm around his neck and helped him down the dark tunnel. Neither one could see how the huge man's face had flushed at the label *monster*. But Holmes was quick on his feet.

"Oh, not at all, dear brother. I am just amazed that after all these years you finally admitted you were fat!"

Mycroft stiffened. Francis felt him shake and then start to spasm as the laughter took hold. It was a good thing that Francis Alparts had the strength of seven men because Mycroft Holmes was laughing so hard, he could barely walk.

Francis mumbled, "I am underground with flames sprouting up and smoke choking me, and I am surrounded by madmen laughing hysterically. Surely I have died and gone to hell."

Holmes' reply was instantaneous as he held the torch high, lighting their steps down the dismal shaft. "Which only goes to prove, as I have consistently stated all along, that you really do have a soul!"

This time it wasn't just Mycroft and Holmes who laughed as they crept along the dark trail.

Thirty minutes later...

A large hand burst through the earth, scattering clods. It was followed by its partner, then the huge head of a giant man. Dirt fell into the hole he had created as he pulled himself up, then reached for two other men also breaking out of the ground. They were covered in mud and grass and old cobwebs, but they were free. Francis sniffed, then turned to see two hundred feet away the Goodwood Derby horse barn engulfed in flames. The pathetic cries of horses locked inside the burning stables added misery to the horror of crackling flames and falling timbers.

As the flames consumed the stables, Holmes saw other men standing closer to the barn, watching closely, waiting for anyone trying to escape the fire. The men carried rifles.

Holmes tapped Francis on the shoulder. Francis nodded, and then slowly they backed further away from the barn.

When they had retreated to the edge of the woods that bordered the Goodwood Derby facility and heard the distant clanging of firemen speeding too late to do any good, Mycroft spoke again. "Now what? I am in need of medical assistance and a place to hide out. But what is your next move, Sherlock? What now?"

Holmes turned to Francis. "Francis, how difficult would it be for you to capture one of those assassins? Can you do it without getting shot? I would prefer it if you could capture the one most likely to be the leader. But, my dear fellow," he put a hand on his giant friend's arm, "I do not want to explain to an irate Jonnie why her beloved husband was shot to pieces. So, is that task doable or not?"

Francis looked back at the group now circling the barn counterclockwise, noting how long it took for each team to make the short circuit. One of the five had pulled away from the others and watched as they patrolled. Francis noticed when the teams disappeared on the opposite side of the flames and how long it took for them to get back. Then he looked at Holmes and said, "I think so. I promise I will take no unnecessary chances, but it will not be without risk."

Sherlock took a deep breath and nodded, and Francis disappeared into the dark. Sherlock and his brother could see the men still circling the flames, but they had grown lackadaisical in their patrol, thinking no one could have survived. They moved to the other side of the barn, which was little more than embers, and then they shouted. Two of them went down immediately and the others fired into the dark, away from where Sherlock and Mycroft stood. The men screamed and then... silence.

Sherlock heard the grumbling of his giant associate approaching in the darkness. "Bloody, puking, ill-bred canker-blossom, stinking mother's son of a brown mullet..." The cursing grew steadily more creative the closer Francis got. "Swag-bellied, pox-marked, fecal-eating..."

"Francis!" Sherlock Holmes exclaimed, hardly able to hold back his laughter. "What if Jonnie could hear you now!"

"What?" He grunted as he dropped a man on the ground at Sherlock's feet like a large sack of potatoes. "Do'na be a'threatening me with my good-natured darling, who's more than capable of scalding the hide of an alligator with nothing but her sweet words. Who, dear sir, da ya think taught me to say what I'm sharing with you now?"

Holmes snorted, and Mycroft grabbed his own belly.

Holmes bent over the unconscious man Francis had dumped on the ground. In the light of the dying flames, he spotted a gold tooth. The man started to stir and Holmes jabbed the handle of his revolver in the man's mouth. "Hold him down, Francis. Grab his face, Mycroft, quickly." Holmes reached into his coat pocket for a handcrafted Barnett Plier-Knife with special blades for everything from wine bottles to emergency surgery. He pried the blade beside the gold tooth and twisted, then grabbed it with the plier's end of the knife and yanked. It popped out. Holmes looked up at Mycroft, who was slowly nodding, his great jowls quivering, and over to Francis, who held the man faster than any iron chain could manage. Holmes returned his knife to his pocket and reached for a small vial, opening it and pouring a couple of drops into his handkerchief and holding that over the man's nose. In a moment he was unconscious again.

Holmes glanced back at Francis, noticing his torn shirt and bloodstained side. "Francis, are you all right?"

"More afraid of Jonnie than this little nick, sir. It bounced off my thick hide but took a piece of me with it. Not the first time, won't be the last. Going to be sore tomorrow. But I'll live. I am in a quandary though..."

Holmes answered his unasked question. "I pulled his tooth before he could bite down on it and kill himself." He held the gold tooth closer to the dying flames. "It's hollow and, with enough pressure applied, will release a poison that quickly kills, thereby keeping the agent from talking under interrogation. The fact that this gentleman has one indicates that he may just have something to be interrogated about."

The next morning in an isolated warehouse in Lamberry, South Sussex

Holmes had borrowed Dr. Watson's mortar and pestle and was grinding away, crushing some type of herb into flour. Jonnie studiously watched, her child on her hip and her baby bump starting to cause her dress to fit a bit snug. Her husband hovered nearby, and Mycroft lay on a large cot with his shirt off and what looked like yards of bandages wrapped around his ponderous belly. His head was stuck in one of his brother's old vellum manuscripts on the subject of medieval poisons. It would have made a lovely family scene reminiscent of a holiday like Thanksgiving or Christmas except for the fact that a man was gagged and tied to a strong chair with ropes and chains and seated in the middle of their industry.

Watson peered over Holmes' other shoulder, and between Jonnie watching from one side and Watson from the other, he was well hemmed in. Suddenly he stopped, scowling from Watson to Jonnie. "Would either of you care to move?"

They jumped back, embarrassed, and Holmes returned to grinding the dry herbs into the finest flour possible. By the time he had finished, Francis stood in front of him, Jonnie back to the right, and Watson in his previous position on Holmes' right hand, his long nose almost stuck into the dried herb.

Mycroft interrupted before Holmes could shoo away his pesty associates. "Brother, are you sure it was the corkwood tree, otherwise known as Duboisia Myoporoides, that you wanted to use as your base element? Because it says here in your own book on poisons that Borrachero, an herb from Ecuador, is also very productive in breaking down the free will of an individual. However, and I quote, 'Effects of ingestion can include paralysis, confusion, heart failure, dry mouth, constipation, tremors, migraine headaches, poor coordination, delusions, visual and auditory hallucinations, and extremely painful death similar to being burned alive.'"

Mycroft's voice had gotten louder and clearer as he spoke with Holmes. The eyes of the dark man strapped to the chair grew round, and sweat broke across his forehead in great beads the more Mycroft spoke.

Holmes turned to his brother. "Yes, Mycroft, I know. But I find it ironic that the drug I am about to inject into this man's veins produces the same effect as the flames would have had on our bodies had we not escaped them. And I can still hear the pathetic screams of those poor horses as the fire consumed them, so I have no pity on this man. He will either tell me what I want to know or..."

Francis shook his head. "I hated being burned at the stake. It took me a decade to recover from those wounds, and for years, every time I sweated, the salt would sting. I remember waking to my own screams, my bed sheets soaked." He turned to the pale man shaking in the chair and whispered in a cold voice, "But that is the fate this one intended for us, so... it's his turn now."

Holmes poured boiling water in the mortar bowl, stirring it into the herbs. He blew on the concoction before placing the syringe in it and vacuuming up the mixture. Then turning to the man seated in front of them, he said, "I don't know your name or care to. You can tell me if you wish. What I want to know is who hired you, where their headquarters are, who was involved in this assassination attempt, and anything else you think might be helpful. Now I am going to inject you with this mixture. It will loosen your tongue. It will also cause it to melt... unless I administer the antidote within an hour of injecting you with this. The name, by the way, of this special brew is Devil's Breath." He ripped off the gag that had held the man mute and asked, "Any questions?"

The man swallowed hard, then gathered his courage and spat at Holmes, "You won't do that. You don't have the guts, Sherlock Holmes."

Jonnie Alparts took the syringe from her boss. She held it up where the prisoner could see and walked toward the bench where Holmes had mixed the brew.

Looking at the man in the chair, she said in a sweetly calm voice, "Watch, please." With that, she pushed the syringe until a small stream ran out onto a plate that held a bar of soap. Immediately, the soap sizzled and hissed. The liquid melted through it, then through the plate and finally onto the wooden table, where it continued to bubble, quickly burning through it. The whole process took forty-five seconds. Then she walked over to the prisoner, stepped behind him, and jabbed him in the neck.

The man screamed. "No! No! Oh Gawd, help me!"

Jonnie walked in front of him, a look of contempt on her face. "You tried to burn my husband and my friends. Now it's your turn. You have about thirty minutes before irrevocable damage is done and you become a paralytic who has full control of his mind and none of his body. You will feel the flames until you finally succumb to the pain, but that will take a while."

The faces of her friends paled. "Jonnie!" Francis cried. "You shouldn't have done that!"

John Watson ran to the man, felt his pulse racing, and placed a hand on his forehead. "He's burning up. Jonnie Alparts, you are a wretched woman! Even a beast would not be so cruel!"

"Dr. Watson, I am as much a beast as I am a woman, and when this soulless bastard has no better ethic than to come after those I love, then he will deal with me and suffer accordingly."

Holmes looked at Jonnie and simply raised an eyebrow. Then he turned to the man trembling in the chair before him. "You do not have long, sir. Who hired you? Start talking now." For the next half hour, the man wept and groaned and talked and talked and talked. Before the interrogation was over, Sherlock and Mycroft knew more than they'd expected to find out and were stunned at the revelations.

"Are you going to help me now?" the man screeched. "Have mercy, sir, mercy. Mercy!"

Holmes shook his head. "That will not be necessary, sir. You have nothing to fear. You were never injected with the liquid that would burn and paralyze you."

"What? She jabbed me in the neck!"

Jonnie, who had been sitting behind the chained man, rose and walked in front of him. She held two syringes in her hand, one full, the other empty. "I am not a beast or a soulless creature. But I am a shrewd one. I injected you with the elements that would loosen your tongue, but not the ones that would melt it."

The man sagged in his seat and wept, and then laughed and snorted. Holmes turned to his stunned associates. "He will not remember a thing after we release him. His memory of the last seventy-two hours will be wiped clean, and he will report back to his masters that the barn burned to the ground with everyone in it."

＊＊＊＊＊＊

Marie's eyes blinked and widened. She didn't know what to make of the man sitting in front of her. He still chuckled, but she wasn't sure that his mirth wasn't deliberate subterfuge. She had dealt with churchmen for over a hundred years, and those relations had never been cordial. The ones she had met, once they discovered she had paranormal abilities, had either wanted to burn her or bed her, neither of which had appealed. Now she was face to face with an enigma.

She realized the pause had grown awkward and Thomas Spurgeon awaited her reply. Finally, she threw off the crocheted blanket and began to rise. The room swam around her, spinning in sick little circles. Her head pounded harder and she sank back into the couch. "Ohhh," she moaned, hands clasping her face. She fell forward and would have landed on her face had Spurgeon not caught her and eased her back onto the couch. She noticed his strength and the disciplined nature of his touch. He was very careful to guard her dignity. She also was very aware that the energy she had first sensed in his handshake resonated powerfully throughout his whole body.

"I would take that a little slower if I were you. Concussions are often hard to recover from. You should be fine in a couple of days, and if you would like, I can send for Mr. Holmes and you can have Dr. Watson examine you. But I assure you it's just a concussion and you will recover."

"How do I know you haven't drugged me? Or intend to hold me prisoner?" she asked.

He tossed his hands in the air and let out a long breath. "I have been repeatedly told to the point of irritation that you are a discerner, that you can read people like a dog-eared book, but that doesn't seem to be the case." He stroked his mustache and continued thoughtfully, "Or if it has been, perhaps the knock on the head and your broken rib have contributed to a diminishing of that gift, because you are certainly not manifesting it now."

Marie avoided looking at him. She opened her mouth, then closed it, a sinking feeling in her stomach.

A knock on the door interrupted the conversation. Thomas Spurgeon answered, "Enter."

A portly older woman, short and wearing a white apron and servant's bonnet, walked in carrying a tray that held sandwiches, a teakettle, and cups. "Good to see ya up, darlin'. I was getting a mite worried, especially with young Tom here a'beaten away at the band. The man doesn't know when to quit, or quite how to treat a special guest, but I'm setting things straight now."

Marie stared for a moment, and then her eyes widened. The nerves in her hands had started to tingle the moment the serving lady crossed the threshold, and now they raged. She didn't know who this woman was, but she felt certain she was a practitioner.

"Hmm, so your discernment *is* working this morning. Very good," Thomas said. "Marie Armont, meet Theodosia Powerscourt. She has been with the organization since the beginning and is, as you have obviously discerned, a gifted woman."

Theodosia curtsied as best she could without spilling the tray. "Marie, it's very simple, dear: some people are born with certain gifts, and it is up to them how they use those gifts. In the old days those people were called prophets and they could be evil or good depending on whom they served. We change names and labels, dear, but that doesn't change substance. The difference between a witch and a prophet is whom they serve."

Marie stopped a sandwich halfway to her mouth. "What? What did you say?"

Theodosia kept on with her lecture, not stopping to answer Marie. "That sounds odd, I know, but it is very true. In the Jewish Testament fifty prophets traveled with Elijah and Elisha so they could be schooled. So, there was an academy, if you will. They carried staffs, and they had the vision where they could see what was going on in other places. They performed amazing acts, miracles if you will, and they could tell when someone was tainted."

Marie's head tilted at the word *taint*. Theodosia explained, "By a demon, dear. Corrupted, controlled, in covenant with? You know that sort of thing."

Marie shuddered, and Thomas' eyebrows rose in surprise.

"Oh, don't worry, Thomas. Any liaison she ever had with any... and it does not appear to have been much..." Theodosia looked down her glasses, scanning Marie from head to toe like a schoolmarm examining a student for lice. "Didn't make much of an impression or leave much of a scar. Yes..." She pointed to Marie's chest as if she were examining an architectural print. "The dark on her soul is her own doing. And even it is in the process of fading." She looked from Thomas back to Marie and addressed her again. "Dearie, you must have been mixing with a better crowd lately because their essence is definitely leaving a mark."

Marie threw her hands up, palms outward. "Stop! Stop it! I don't believe any of this," she barked. "You are telling me that I'm not a witch, that the Old Testament had people in it just like me. That gifts don't determine wicked bent, that the person does, and that you are part of an organization that has been aware of this for... for how long?"

"Hundreds?" Thomas began, then shrugged.

"More like thousands, dear," Theodosia corrected, picking up the tray.

"I know what I have done. I know I have cast spells; I know I have killed people and I have stolen things and I have..." She was about to say *committed immoral acts*, but looked at Thomas and shifted to "done things that I am ashamed of." She paused and her arrogance tried to cover her shame. "And not ashamed of!"

Thomas looked her square in the eye and almost said *we*, but changed to "I know... but what hasn't occurred to you is that we—our organization—has been in the restoration business for a very, very long time. None of us," the way he said *us* told Marie that he included himself in the statement, "have anything to brag about and all of us have much we deeply regret." Unconsciously his fingers traced the scar that framed his face. "What we need to know, what I need to know, is not what you have been, Marie, but what you want to be. We are an old and large organization that has been fighting against the families... Masters... whatever misnomer they want to claim now, and recently things have heated up. A war is coming, maybe more than one, and when they are over, the world will be a very different place, for better or for worse."

"And you want me to turn on the Masters and help you?"

"You already have, dear," Theodosia chirped. "We just want to know if you wish to survive?"

******

Robbie Scott whistled as he kicked a can down the cobblestone alley. For the first time in his life he had a brand-new pair of shoes that actually fit him and matched. His mother was on the mend, his belly was full, and he was happy. As he made the next turn in the back alley where he often played with his friends, he failed to notice two men lurking behind him. He kicked the can and watched it slam into the old brick wall, almost hitting the circle he had chalked as a target. *Oh well,* he thought. *I'll get it next time.* A shadow loomed over him; two large hands grabbed him while another placed a handkerchief filled with ether over his nose. He struggled briefly, then slipped into darkness.

Later that night...

The large room opened to the sky. At just the right time of year, the full moon would look down through the opening and weep over the horrible activities occurring beneath it. Tonight, forty crimson-robed men stood in a semicircle around a great horned idol—Molech, the horrible demon god the Canaanites worshiped, a god that good men had tried to banish for centuries and evil ones worshiped in the dark crevices of the night. The idol was ten feet tall and made of a dark blood-red stone imported from Eastern Europe. A large granite table lay at its feet. A horn jutted from each corner of the stained table. Chains were welded to the horns, and held by those chains was a small boy.

Between the table and the encircling men was another circle. In it were twelve men and women, their backs and buttocks streaked with whip cuts and blood dripping down their legs. They also were manacled. At the stroke of midnight, a drum began to beat and the worshipers began to chant. The men and women in the inner circle whimpered, and the high priest walked out from the center of the forty robed men. He carried a flaming torch and a huge jagged knife. The wicked knife glistened, but it was the torch that held the pain. The idol was not just a statue; it was also a furnace. The priest halted in front of the huge idol and quickly raised his hands. The chanting stopped; only the drum continued to beat.

The priest cried out in a frenzied dark tongue he had not learned but the darkness inside him was intimately acquainted with. Then he took the torch and lit the furnace, the table began to heat, and the child on it screamed.

Early the next morning...

The delivery man knocked on the door of 221B Baker Street. He held a wooden box the size of a woman's bonnet. Mrs. Hudson opened the door, signed for the delivery, and took the box up the stairs to Holmes' apartment. Holmes answered the door, his ever-present pipe billowing. Taking the box, he laid it on the table and walked over to check on Bob, nestled in his crib away from home. The boy was closing in on two years old. The Alparts family spent so much time with Holmes that he had invested in some furniture for them. Not that they couldn't afford whatever suited them; he just wanted to contribute. So, the age-old bachelor flat was now trimmed in fancy curtains, and one bedroom was set aside for the Alparts family or Watson when he chose to visit. Bob's crib held the place of honor next to the small icebox that Holmes had also installed for when Bob or Jonnie needed a snack.

As Holmes checked on Bob and opened the icebox out of habit, Jonnie came in from the bedroom, where Francis' snores rumbled, causing the walls to vibrate. She took the mandatory earplugs out of her ears and then noticed the box. Frowning, she drew closer to it and sniffed. "Mr. Holmes, were you expecting a delivery of meat?"

Stiffening, Holmes closed the icebox and stared at the package that sat on Watson's desk. "No, I was not. Perhaps you should take Bob for a morning walk, or something, and it might also be a good idea to wake Francis. I may be in need of him shortly."

Jonnie's head tilted and then her eyes widened. She grabbed the sleeping child and said, "I'll rouse the beast and then I will go check in on Mrs. Hudson."

Holmes didn't bother to answer but took out his penknife and cut the strings on the box. Jonnie rushed out the door, and Francis lumbered out of the bedroom, his clothes rumpled and his hair standing on end. "Jonnie said you might have need of me, sir. And then she started crying and ran out the door with Bob. What's going on?"

"We had a delivery. Jonnie smelled blood, and considering the size of the box I am concerned about its contents. I suppose I could have let you sleep on, but..."

"Think nothing of it, Mr. Holmes. Times like this are what God made friends for. Do you want me to open it? Or do you think we should take it out back in case it contains some deadly thing?"

Holmes scratched his chin, frowned, and sighed. "I don't think that will be necessary."

Francis carefully picked up the box and drew it to his face. He took a deep breath and then winced. "No explosives that I can smell, sir, but..."

Holmes looked up at him and finished his sentence. "Human blood. There is an eighty-seven percent chance it is a human head. Perhaps a day old, and since it was mailed to me, it is probably someone I know, most probably someone I care about. That narrows the possibilities down considerably. Since I know where you are and I saw Watson leave earlier this morning, and I know that Mycroft is bolted inside the stone walls of an old castle, and since the box does not weigh as much as a fully formed adult would..." Holmes' voice cracked, and he whispered, "That leaves only one viable choice."

Francis put his hand on his friend's shoulder. Holmes' eyes glistened. Francis' own eyes watered as he realized Holmes was right. For, now that he had been given a sense of whom it could be, he recognized the scent of the small street urchin, Robbie Scott. "I will take care of him, sir. We don't have to open this box. It won't serve any good purpose. Now that you have narrowed it down for me, I am sure that the blood I smell in the box belongs to Robbie."

Holmes shuddered as the truth clicked into the niche he had made for it. He sighed deeply. "I think we have to because if the villains responsible for this abomination are true to form, they will leave a note, and that may hold a clue." With that Holmes started to open the box.

The huge man put his large hand over Holmes' own. "Aye, sir, the box may have to be opened, but you are not the one that has to open it. I will do it."

Holmes saw merciful determination in his friend's face and nodded. He backed off and sat in the chair facing away from the box. A few moments later, Francis closed the box and handed Holmes a blood-stained note. It was only one word: *Next?*

******

Marie felt a breath of cold on her arm. She pulled it back under the crocheted blanket. Thomas Spurgeon and Theodosia Powerscourt had both retired earlier. It had been a long day of questions and debate, and finally of resolution. She still didn't trust them, but then she never trusted anyone; she couldn't believe they trusted her. So that made them even. They had, however, agreed to work together against the Masters, specifically the ones who had caused the stampede in Surrey Court and killed a dozen worshipers. But now they were gone and it was late, and her head was hurting again. She pulled the blankets up around her neck, and then she heard him.

"Arright now, ma'am. Yer need ter wake up. The bleedin' gatekeeper told me I can't get in until I take yer somewhere, so, please, if yer would be so kind, wake up."

Marie's eyes shot open and she jumped off the couch. In front of her stood a small boy dressed in new clothes, a smart-looking cap, and polished shoes. Her eyes narrowed; then she frowned. Though smiling, the young man looked a bit embarrassed. She tilted her head, confused. Then it hit her. He was dead. She was looking at the ghost of a child. Her mouth dropped open and her eyes shuttered. A haunting was the last thing she had expected here.

The boy understood her confusion and answered, "I'm bloody well a bit bewildered meself, ma'am. One minute I were kickin' a can dahn the alley in me new shoes, and the bloomin' next I were... well, I don't remember the next... then I were standin' before this tall man bigger even than Francis Alparts, and 'e said I 'ad ter show yer sumfin before 'e could let me in. And, ma'am, I got a glimpse behind them gates wen the big man weren't a'lookin', and I would right like ter go in, so if yer could 'elp me?"

Marie struggled to comprehend the young man's English. When he mentioned Francis Alparts, things really muddled. Alparts worked for Holmes. And if this boy knew him... then she needed to contact Holmes and let him know and... then what? Well, she would just have to work it out on the fly. She looked down on the child and asked, "What's your name, boy?"

"Robbie Scott, ma'am. My name is Robbie Scott."

"So, you know Sherlock Holmes?"

"Yes, ma'am, I worked for Mr. Holmes. He gave me a half sovereign just last week, when I gave him a message from his brother, Mycroft Holmes." Robbie shook his head slowly when he mentioned Mycroft. "That is a very fat man, goodness."

"Yes, well..." Marie snorted at the child's comment. The boy hadn't known many days in his short life where he had a full belly, much less a ponderous one, and Mycroft's obesity was a novelty to him.

"Robbie, you and I are going to see Mr. Holmes. And then we will see what he has to say about things, and where we head to next. Is that all right with you?"

"Sure, it is, ma'am. I like Mr. Holmes and he always has a meal and money for me...and me mum." The boy's head lowered and he stared at the floor. "But I suppose I won't be needing that now, will I. And what about me mum? What will happen to her?"

Marie put her hand beneath his chin and lifted his head. "Robbie, didn't you tell me that you had met a big man at the gates and snuck a peek inside?"

"Yes, ma'am, I did! And it was bootifull!"

"Well, I have it on good authority that those gates are extending and that land is increasing, and one day it will pour over into this one and all the woes and horrors of this earth will be swallowed up behind those marvelous gates. You have seen them; do you have any doubt that they are stronger and able to subdue this world?"

Robbie sighed and looked up at Marie. He scrunched up his face in what he assumed was a philosophical pose and answered, "Aye, ma'am, I know it's true, but it seems to be taking an awful long time. And you know what else?"

"What else?" Marie asked softly, amazed at her own speech and now completely engulfed in the conversation.

"The timing on that expansion... is up to us, ain't it?"

His response shocked her and sent a flood of despair and guilt over her, drowning her in the dark pain of the sharp words. Robbie hugged her. "But Miss Marie, you don't need to be sad...cause this is your time...for just such a time as this have you entered the kingdom."

The impact of the boy's declaration hit Marie, overwhelming her, tossing her like a toy boat in a squall. She fell on her face, tears soaking the floor as she bent over and wept. Her sobs wracked her, cleansing her, draining her of all bitterness and resentment and layers and layers of embedded guilt. Finally, her quivering chin stilled, her breath returned, and her heart quit aching. Rising from the floor, she tried to wipe the wrinkles from her crumpled dress. Then she gulped a deep cleansing breath and straightened. She smiled at Robbie, grabbed his hand, and together they walked out of the library.

******

Mycroft rumbled through the ancient halls of the Castle Conway, bored, sore, and determined to exercise if it killed him. As he was walking to keep from boredom, he became bored with walking. His mind raced like it always did. But this time the race was focused down a razor-thin line. He was mentally filing and comparing the names given by the man they had interrogated. Mycroft admitted that most of the names were the products of speculation on the criminal's part. The idea was if a person the criminal knew was definitely connected with the Masters and therefore with the attempt on their lives, then the people under that individual were also connected. And that was troubling, especially when the trail led down its sullied way, ending with Detective Lestrade of Scotland Yard, who had worked with Mycroft's brother on many occasions and was known as an honest, if not always astute, man.

Mycroft could not imagine Lestrade being involved with the ploys of the Masters. But... he scratched his substantial chin and lit a cigar as he considered the next idea. He could imagine Lestrade being duped and used by someone over him with authority to move Lestrade like an unwitting pawn. Mycroft grunted and reached for a treacle tart, then thought better of it. He looked back at it glistening in the pie plate, grabbed it, and stuffed it in his mouth, continuing his line of thought. What if he knew who was involved? What could they do? Obviously, the Masters feared they could do something, or else why have them assassinated? What was it that the Masters feared?

Mycroft closed his eyes and settled back into his overstuffed chair, his mind marching forward like a colossal juggernaut, an unstoppable steamroller flattening every piece of data into a smooth highway of information that could be ridden over to whatever objective he desired. This whole state of affairs had come into being because of the discovery of gold in the Langlaagte region of the Witwatersrand Basin and Cecil Randolph the diamond magnate's desire to own his own country. Gold would change the balance of world power. Mycroft supported England, at least for the most part, because when he did not he could complain loudly and persistently and pound on the desks of whatever petty tyrant was interested in filling his pockets at the expense of the downtrodden. What the Masters hated was publicity, exposure, and any thwarting of their control, and Mycroft's and Sherlock's movements for the common man in London threatened all of those.

Mycroft slammed his ham-like fist on the table. He knew all of that. So, what had pushed them to come after him? What specific event, or threat of action, did he know or could he influence that they despised? What was it? Mycroft's wound ached, and his exercise, limited as it was, exhausted him. The foreign and unfamiliar feelings of helplessness combined with the sugar he had just gulped down caused him to be sleepy, and soon the giant man slipped into unconsciousness.

Tentacles, hundreds of octopus-like tentacles each with a dozen suckers, lashed at him and ripped his flesh, sucking the lifeblood from him. Every time he struck with his sword or crushed one in his fists, others arose to take their place. He was wrestling underwater, gasping for breath, the air forced from him by the tentacles of the giant beast he fought. Suddenly the appendages tugged him toward the sharp-toothed maw of the beast. He thrashed against the tow, grappling vainly against the unrelenting drag. His blood flowed from a hundred wounds, and then the head of the creature loomed before him, mouth opened like the dark gates of a razor-sharp hell.

He awoke. His body, covered in sweat, quivered, but he now knew what his magnificent brain had not been able to communicate while awake; it had broken through while he slept. A precise tactical strike could sever the beast's head. Mycroft chuckled as he reached for another treacle tart.

******

A sharp knock at the street entrance of 221B brought Mrs. Hudson, with Jonnie a pace behind her, to answer it. Jonnie had her child in one hand and a large butcher knife in the other. She had snatched it as they raced out of the kitchen for the door. Jonnie and Mrs. Hudson had become great friends, Mrs. Hudson eventually confiding in Jonnie that she was aware of much more than Holmes or Dr. Watson had suspected. Jonnie's troubled look of the morning and her unusual trip to the kitchen had drawn up Mrs. Hudson's suspicions from the bottom of her deep well of intuition and ended with Jonnie spilling her fears of the dark package. So, when the sharp rap of an unexpected visitor knocked on the door, both of them were concerned, Jonnie with the knife and child and Mrs. Hudson with a small revolver tucked behind her in her apron string.

Mrs. Hudson drew a long breath and Jonnie tensed; the knocking continued. Mrs. Hudson opened the door, a counterfeit smile etched on her face. Marie Armont stood at the entrance with a grim look plastered across her beautiful features. Her eyes were red and swollen, and her arm hung at her side at a strange angle, almost as if she held the hand of a child. Jonnie blinked and looked again.

This time she saw the translucent figure of Robbie Scott standing at Marie's side, holding her hand.

Mrs. Hudson did not see the child but heard Jonnie's gasp. "What, Jonnie? What ails you?"

Jonnie just shook her head, then placed her hand on her baby bump.

Mrs. Hudson nodded. "Oh yeah, not good to get too excited too quickly." Jonnie and Mrs. Hudson both knew Marie. "Come in, child. You look as though ya seen a ghost. Get up now to see Mr. Holmes, and if you like I will send for Dr. Watson."

Marie swallowed hard, Mrs. Hudson's ironic statement stunning her. She shook her head. "I will be all right, dear lady. Just been a difficult two days, but I have urgent business with Mr. Holmes, and if you don't mind?"

"Not at all. Go on up."

Jonnie followed behind Marie, her eyes never wavering from Robbie, who had winked at her. Her two-year-old, who loved to play with Robbie, had also noticed the small apparition and giggled at him.

Marie knocked on Holmes' door and was quickly greeted by the detective. "Marie, what a surprise!" Then Holmes saw Robbie and fell to his knees, his chest pounding, lips quivering. "Robbie!" he whispered.

"Hi, Mr. 'olmes. I bet yer did not fink yer would be seein' me anytime soon, did yer?"

Holmes laughed in spite of himself. He glanced back at the box and then to the boy in front of him. "No, Robbie, I am afraid I did not." Then he looked up at Marie, grabbed the doorknob, and pulled himself to his feet. "And I did not expect to see you either, Marie, and I certainly in all my days did not expect to see you together."

Jonnie had joined her towering husband, and together they had watched Holmes greet his visitors.

Robbie looked up at the giant man. "Hi ya, guvnor. I met a man that made yer look short. He guards the gate ter the wonderful city, and 'e sent me to fetch you to 'elp yer and Mr. 'olmes and Mrs. Jonnie and Marie find the... the chuffin'... men 'oo..." He shook his head and shifted thoughts. "I don't remember wot they did exactly, but the big man 'oo guarded the gate told me that I were ter sic yer on them and yer would sort it out. So, ah, I wound up wiv Miss Marie 'ere at Tom's place and brought 'er ter ya. 'Cause it's gonna take all of yer ter put this straight."

Jonnie sat on the couch and patted the seat beside her. She noticed that Robbie's clothes were spotless and gleaming. His shoes matched and his typically unruly hair was combed beneath the stylish cap he wore.

He accepted her invitation and curled up beside her. "You are so pretty, Mrs. Jonnie. You're beautiful."

Jonnie beamed, but then sadness shook her back to the reality that she was talking to a ghost whose mortal head was wrapped in a box on the table.

Marie sensed Jonnie's struggle and sat next to Robbie. "And that's the thanks I get for holding your hand all the way from Tom's to here, watching out for you when you crossed the road and all?"

"Oh, Miss Marie, I wasn't slighting you by pointing out Mrs. Jonnie's beauty. Not at all, ma'am." Robbie's speech had improved significantly since he had entered Holmes' quarters; he was mindful he was surrounded by the educated and didn't want to look ignorant to them. "I just didn't want to go on about it at Tom's."

Marie frowned. She had no clue where the boy was heading...

Oblivious to the heartstrings he was strumming, Robbie blundered on, "You... know!" He rolled his eyes with a *come on, lady, help me here* nod as if trying to keep a secret.

"Know what, Robbie?" she asked, suspicions beginning to surface.

"Why, Miss Marie, I didn't want to make Thomas Spurgeon jealous!"

Marie's eyes widened. She was caught between *I don't think so* and *Really?!* and couldn't decide whether to be indignant or blush.

Jonnie didn't hide her laughter well on good days, and this was not a good day. The couch shook, and then Francis joined his bride and the room rocked with laughter. The only person making any semblance of hiding his laughter was Holmes, and even then, it twinkled from his eyes. Marie sat stunned on the couch, her mouth open but nothing coming forth. The faint hint of a smile tried to creep across her face, but she quickly tucked it away.

"Well then..." Holmes grabbed the awkward moment and moved forward. "What can you tell us that will help us sort this out, Robbie?"

"Well, Mr. Holmes, here is what I remember. It was a very big room, and it had a high window in it where the full moon beat down. The window was open and I could smell the sea breeze and even the scent of fish. I also remember the room held about a hundred people and had large iron beams holding the roof up. It seemed to be walled in and not really open, almost like it was hidden from the rest of a larger hall, if you know what I mean?"

Holmes nodded.

The boy continued, "And it had a smokestack that shot up out of the room. The stack was attached to the furnace."

"Furnace?" Francis asked.

"Yeah, you know where they burned the bodies?" the boy quipped innocently.

The large man gulped back unexpected bile and just nodded to the ghost that had intimate experience with the furnace.

"Anything else? Anything at all, Robbie?" Marie whispered, her face hot with tears. She noticed Robbie's image starting to fade. He had accomplished his mission of fetching them and was moving on.

"Oh yeah, there was one other thing..." The boy's voice sounded far away, his spectral body now just a haze.

"What, Robbie?" Jonnie and Marie gasped in chorus.

"There was a big eye carved over the stone doorway, and it was in the middle of a triangle." And then from very far away they heard Robbie laugh. "Now would you look at that. Who woulda thought?" And he was gone.

******

Mycroft felt good. He sat in his carriage, finally out of that dreary old castle. He had hit upon the perfect plan to draw out the leadership and most of the members of the Witwatersrand Basin gold cabal, or family, whichever it was. He had paced for days, and then finally in a fitful dream it had occurred to him he must change his approach. He must give his enemies what they wanted, but not the way they expected it. It must be a trap within a trap. They would see through the first phase, but would they realize there was a second one? Well, he would soon know.

The carriage rolled to a stop in front of the Diogenes Club. The Diogenes Club, of which Mycroft was a founding member, was a socializing place for the wealthy men of London who did not wish to socialize, whether from acute forms of shyness or simply the selfish egocentrism that often accompanies the pampered privileged from birth. They did not wish to be bothered breathing the same air as their fellows. Yet they loved comfort and the latest publications, whether monthlies or the daily *Times*. The rules were simple: no member was allowed to take notice of any other member. There was absolutely no talking, and if these rules were broken it would be brought to the notice of the committee and immediate expulsion would result. Typically, the air was thick with cigar smoke and the quiet hum of the newly introduced ceiling fans.

The carriage dipped as Mycroft stepped on the threshold and then down onto the pavement. The springs snapped back as soon as his ponderous weight was removed. Then he climbed gradually, step by step, up the granite staircase to the large wooden doors that opened on the bastion of aristocratic British elitism. Mycroft did not expect too many to notice his entrance. It was actually considered inappropriate for any member to acknowledge another. But he did take note when a few papers shifted and narrowed eyes peered over their edges.

A knowing smile found a willing place upon his lips. And then he did the most outrageous thing. He shouted, "I am alive and I have a list of names, many of which will sound familiar, very familiar. I am going to hand that list to Billy Stead, and he will publish it in his *Pall Mall Gazette*... and then all the world will know your names and your plan. Unless?" An eerie, angry silence flowed like a stagnant fog, filling the old rooms with its menace. Mycroft, expecting such a reaction, shuffled toward his preferred oversized chair, unfolded a London *Times*, and pretended to read the paper while smoking his favorite cigar.

Five minutes later a waiter stood in front of him. Mycroft pulled his paper down and looked at the tray the waiter held. On it lay a folded note. He picked it up and read, *What do you want?*

Mycroft scribbled *I want in. If I cannot defeat you, I will join you* on the note, refolded it, and placed it back on the tray, then continued reading his paper. A few minutes later the butler returned. Mycroft took the note and read, *Under one condition. Bring us the head of Sherlock Holmes.*

******

"I thought I had a foolproof scheme to trap them— gather them all together and then throw the net around them and haul them in. But—and it troubles me to admit this—they outwitted me. They asked something of me that I cannot do, and they know it. Or at least I think they do." Mycroft was still wheezing from the exertion of climbing his brother's stairs and trying to catch his breath and sip on a gin and tonic at the same time. Sherlock sat in his normal seat and puffed on his pipe. Watson cleaned his tools from the day's use; Marie hovered near, watching with keen interest.

Holmes steepled his long fingers and asked, "So what was it, Mycroft? What did they ask of you?"

The huge man looked his brother in the eye. "They want your head on a platter, or at least in a box."

Sherlock's response was limited to raising one eyebrow. An anxious silence flowed between them. More brainpower was used in that time than would ever be again until the invention of the analytical engine's cousin a half century later. Then Sherlock Holmes shifted into the far-off look that Watson was well acquainted with. His brother had been awaiting its arrival, scrutinizing every twitch and every frown.

When Sherlock shifted, Mycroft roared, "Brother, you cannot seriously be considering... It's too much, man. If you are gone, who takes up your mantle? Who has your gifts, your experience, your connections?"

Holmes cast a long, slow glance at his friends, then stopped at his brother. "Thank you, Mycroft. But it might just be time."

Marie gasped and broke into French, cursing his stupidity and foolish English pride. *"Espece d'ane idiot. Tes cerveaux sont des crottes, arrete, cette folie Maudite!* You arrogant Englishman, do you think that you are like the Christ? Heh? No, you are not! One sacrifice is sufficient; there need be no other! And what of Robbie?" Although, considering her mood, it came out *Roobiiee.* "Do not diminish the street child's sacrifice by adding your own." She balled her small hands into fists and stood over him, threatening to pound him. "This is an outlandish request! And you are... are..." She launched into French again. *"Espece d'ane idiot* for considering it!"

Holmes crossed his legs, hands curled around his pipe. He looked up at her and laughed, thinking, *I am glad that the Alpartses are out for the evening because Jonnie would have sided with Marie and the wallpaper would have peeled beneath their combined onslaught.*

He sighed and looked back at Watson, Marie, and Mycroft. "But my mind is made up." In a whisper as hard as shipyard iron he said, "If my head is what it takes, then that is a cheap price to pay."

Holmes' brother paled. His great jowls hung open and he was unable to reply. Finally, he shook his head vigorously and cried, "Bloody hell, Sherlock, what is wrong with you? I agree with Marie; you are *espece d'ane idiot...* outrageous, absurd, not necessary, a foolish waste, did I say outrageous?!"

"Uh yes, I believe you did. But I have examined the situation and discarded several different alternatives. This is the only one that will get you through the gate into the inner circles and gather the hosts where they can be brought down in one fell swoop, and if my head is what it takes to bring it about…" He whispered, his voice cracking, "I willingly offer it, brother. But I will not ask you to be here for the act. That duty will fall on others."

He looked at Watson, who grimaced and joined Marie's cursing. "You are a bloody fool, Holmes, if you think for one minute that I will participate in your… your damn bloody decapitation!"

Mycroft knew his brother and realized once his mind was made up there was no turning back. So, he stood up on shaky legs, took one final look at his brother, eyes glistening, and walked out of the apartment, down the stairs, and out to the street. Sherlock went to the window and watched, standing back far enough that an outside observer could not see him. His brother looked like he had aged years and stood at the corner, his kerchief wiping his eyes. He called a cab and carefully boarded. Holmes noticed two men watching his brother. They also called a cab and quickly followed Mycroft.

Sherlock turned to his angry associates. "Now the deed must be done, and I cannot do it myself. And I have a message I need you to deliver, Marie."

Three hours later at Thomas Spurgeon's office

"I didn't expect to see you so soon," Thomas Spurgeon said, the corners of his lips giving way to a slight smile.

Amused, Marie's own face betrayed an invitation that refused to let him look away. "But here I am." Her eyes locked on his, unconsciously scouring his handsome face for something she hadn't yet realized she was looking for.

"Indeed you are, Marie Armont." His smirk widened into a full smile. "And how may I assist you?" His hand reached out to shake hers as he invited her into his office.

She slipped her hand into his and felt the strength of the man's body and, better yet, the mystical current of his soul. She was not aware that he had also sensed the life stream running through her, nor did she notice how his heart pounded at her touch.

She sat on the couch and began, "Mr. Holmes sent me to ask for your help. He seems to think that we will soon be involved in violent exploits against a very dark foe and that your help might be desirable."

"Desirable?" He frowned, curiosity in his voice.

"He actually said, and I quote, 'Don't let that damn preacher turn you down, Marie. We need him and his men, and you have to persuade him his aid is indispensable.'"

"Hmmm. Well, in that case, what does he want? And why does he think I have access to resources that the Yard, or others, might be better prepared to provide?"

"He didn't say. He only assumes you do, and it has been my observation that he rarely misjudges people. But I must admit I do wonder about asking someone committed to keeping peace and loving their enemies for help in what we know will end, and actually plan to end, in violence."

Spurgeon got up from his comfortable chair and paced with the stealthy grace Marie had once witnessed in a lion at London's Zoological Gardens.

"I am a man of peace, Marie. I follow the Prince of Peace and absolutely believe in showing mercy to those who consider themselves my enemies. But I am also aware that Mr. Holmes' request reflects a level of sacrifice that I don't know, if it were laid on me, I could rise to. But I am convinced both in mind by physical evidence and in spirit by a more dependable substance that those he seeks to punish are given over, as in totally consumed with darkness. If they even retain a soul is debatable, and if my father were here he would call me into question for saying that... But I said it and do honestly wonder about it." He stopped pacing and turned toward her, skewering her with an unflinching gaze. The hair on her neck stood up, and she recoiled beneath the fire from his eyes.

"Those who claim they know the Prince of Peace and see Him as a gentle ever-suffering lamb forget or never knew that He has another face and another name. They don't call Him the Lion for nothing, Marie, and even though He endures great suffering, He also told His disciples to sell their cloaks and buy a sword."

Her bewildered response caused his eyebrow to shoot up. "What?"

She clamped her mouth shut, then slowly loosened it. "Several things come to mind. But first, how did you know about Mr. Holmes' plans and about his enemy? And second, how do you balance the warrior and the priest? That seems to be a conflict that would tear a heart to pieces."

Thomas eased back into his chair and studied his fingers. After a long moment he raised his eyes; the warmth was back as well as the gentleness that seemed to be his undergirding.

"I got this scar," he pointed to the red streak that framed his handsome face, "in a war that scarred my soul as well as my face. When I was younger, I learned the art of war, and I was extremely good at it. My reputation was such that when there was a hard task, or one from which everyone else shied away, I stepped forward. It was on one such mission, when those with me were cut down and my men were all wounded, and I was bleeding and blinded by the sword stroke that left this scar, that I saw something through the bloody tears and heard something through the shrieking curses of war. I saw a man. His eyes were like flame and I could barely stand to look at Him, but He would not allow me to look away. He held my gaze and fixed it, and His gaze burned me. I screamed with the agony of the flames that rippled through my body. His words were, 'You are My soldier now, but only My battles, only My enemies.' And then He said, 'Two swords—one in My mouth and the other in your hand.' Then He was gone. I looked around me, and the enemy was gone and only the groans of my wounded men pierced the stillness. Since then I have engaged in violence only upon command, and there have been many times where that word did not come. And times when I didn't think it would that it did."

As he spoke, the world around them slowed into a sluggish dream. She could barely hear. She felt waves of heat and sorrow, mixed with a fire of something she had encountered before but always run from. She felt holiness, unadulterated holiness; not the artificial rigidity of sterile regulation but the living flame of righteousness that exposed every motivation and turned shades of grey into the black and white threads that so easily entangled her heart. Waves of it rushed through her, ripping away dark veils and healing brokenness she had made peace with but limped through life because of. Then she heard, "Will you go with this man?" And then again with such intensity she could barely move her whole body, shaking beneath the thunder of the question, "Will you go with Thomas?"

She bowed her head, her breath coming in gasps. She nodded vigorously, and then heard her own voice shout, as if she was far removed, "Yes!"

At the sound of her yes, the slow-motion spin stopped. She blinked and found herself standing face to face with Thomas. He stared down at her; their bodies so close they could feel the heat from their shared experience diminishing. He moved his hand to her face and brushed it across her cheek. She leaned in closer, her lips resting inches from his. Then he let out a puff of air and chuckled.

"What?" she asked, her heart lighter than she had ever known.

"Well," he continued, "I am not sure, but I think we just set a record."

She pulled back, a gentle smile on her lips, curiosity brimming from her beautiful eyes. "For what?"

He laughed again, drawing her close to him. "For the shortest courtship, my dear!"

Her brilliant smile and warm embrace told him all he wanted to know. Then she pulled back and looked up with an expression he was to grow extremely familiar with, one that could pry the secrets out of granite statues and lesser men. With an eyebrow cocked and an accent now dipped in French, she purred, "But, my dear Thomas, you have not answered the second question. How did you know Holmes' plans?"

Thomas Spurgeon threw back his head and laughed. "You'll have to learn to listen, my dear girl." Her expression coaxed the next phrase from him. "Oh, you don't know what for. Why, that is simple: the music, my dear, learn to listen for the music."

A frown lit on her features but was quickly swept away by a kiss. She thought, *He thinks he has a secret.*

And he thought, *I will keep it as long as I can, but I don't think I can hold out under a great siege.* And then they both stopped thinking.

A day later at Holmes' apartment

Jonnie and Francis both paced the length of Sherlock's parlor. "This is foolish, absurd. If you think for one minute just because of our sordid past that we can participate in this bloody and self-destructive scheme of yours, then you are a bigger fool than I thought, Sherlock Holmes!" This time it was not Jonnie Alparts who was ranting but her very large and very red-faced husband. He had started to see Holmes as a father figure, and when Holmes had told him about the demand made on Mycroft by the Masters and his intent to accommodate it, Francis had objected loudly and fervently, and in several different languages that even Marie didn't know, what a foolish idea it was. Finally, when he had screamed himself hoarse and Mrs. Hudson had knocked on the door, frantic to call the police, and when Holmes had finished his pipe, he sat down in an exhausted huff and simply said, "I won't do it!"

Holmes looked over at Watson and then at Marie, who had remained strangely quiet during Francis' rant. Jonnie had felt and tried to communicate to her husband that not all was as it appeared, but he wouldn't hear her because of his fear of losing Holmes. Watson stood shaking his head in dislike and shuffled into the back room.

As he did, Holmes put his hand on his giant friend's knee and said, "Francis, hear me out. You don't have to take my head... as a matter of fact, that would be a bit redundant. You see, I have already done it."

Watson reentered the den and placed a hat-sized box on Francis' lap. The lid was open and Francis peered inside. Jonnie jumped over to stare as well. She gasped, and Francis took one look and started laughing. "You old schemer, you deceptive snake, how did you manage this?"

Jonnie's response was colder. "Mr. Holmes, you let your brother think you would go through with this? You let him leave this room in torment? How could you?"

Holmes' smile at Francis' statement turned to a self-condemning one at Jonnie's. "Two questions, two answers. First Francis' answer. Have you ever heard of Madame Tussaud's wax museum? They make wax masks and mannequins of historical characters and celebrities. They even use human hair, and thanks to Dr. Watson's skillful use of resources drawn from a local slaughterhouse, this particular specimen has very authentic parts. And thanks again to Watson's skills"—he motioned to the good doctor, who nodded in appreciation— "those parts are installed in this very authentic facsimile and will include, at his suggestion, which by the way only proves his profession is not yet far removed from the leeches of a century past, my own blood."

"And the second question?" Jonnie reminded him.

Holmes was about to reply but Marie interrupted him. "It's called plausible deniability. The Masters employ witches who would know if Mycroft was involved in a ruse. So, he must not know, for his own sake as well as the plan's."

Jonnie frowned but shook her head. "He is your brother, sir, and he will not be happy with you afterwards."

"I am afraid that is so, Jonnie, but he will be alive to foster that anger, will he not?" Holmes sighed, then changed subjects. "Now we have an attack to plan. There will be approximately seventy-five to a hundred men gathered in the hall, and there are only five of us, so the success of this enterprise depends on surprise and duplicity, and of course the Alpartses' gift of strength and carnage."

"And mine," Marie added, pulling a wicked-looking dagger from out of nowhere.

"And mine." Watson brandished a sawed-off shotgun, which had a brilliant mechanic alter to hold a round drum containing fifty shells.

"And my own." Holmes placed a small ball-sized object made of steel and full of flechettes on the table.

******

On the night of the full moon, Mycroft Holmes stood at the doors of the Thames Ironworks and Shipbuilding Company. The dock was busy with wagons coming and going, drunks and the homeless ambling along the sidewalk, and a very badly tuned Salvation Army band playing beneath a gaslight across the street. A large Masonic eye centered in a carpenter's compass was etched in the arch over the doors. On the left side of the doors hung a bronze placard that read *Home of Riverside and General Laborers' Union*. Two burly men stood guard beneath the flickering gaslights that framed the large door. They were dressed in dark blazers and trousers, and had bowler-type steed derbies pulled down over their faces. Their large unkempt muttonchops did not hide the cold glare that held Mycroft motionless while they examined the contents of the large hatbox he carried.

Mycroft had not opened the box when Francis had handed it to him. He'd simply placed it on the leather seat at his side in the carriage while striving to hold the contents of his stomach at bay. He had fortified himself with several rounds of scotch and was grateful to Providence for it. The guard had obviously been waiting for Mycroft. As soon as he saw him, he knocked on the double doors behind him, and a professional-looking man, who Mycroft assumed was a physician, stepped out. He unwrapped the box and held the contents up by the hair. Mycroft turned his head and leaned against the door, barely able to keep his bile behind his teeth.

The physician saw the severed neck, noticed the trailing esophagus, and smelled the blood. He nodded to the guards, who closed the box and handed it back to Mycroft. Mycroft's hands shook so badly he could barely hold the box. The guard looked on unsympathetically and motioned to the door, holding it open for Mycroft. As soon as he passed over the threshold, he felt the dark soul-dampening chill that typically accompanied occult events.

Another man waited, wearing a red robe trimmed in gold and fastened with black buttons. A hood shadowed his face. "This way, please. You will be required to wait until the appropriate time." The man walked down a short hall, turned left, and escorted Mycroft into a room with two overstuffed leather chairs. "I shall return when it is time."

Mycroft did not think it possible to be terrified sitting in an enclosed room, waiting to meet with a secret society of demon worshipers with your brother's head in a box at your side, and still fall asleep. But he did. A fierce knock on the door startled him awake as several robed and hooded men walked into the room to accompany him to his initiation.

Only one of them spoke. "Come with us."

Mycroft nodded, his jowls shaking, and followed them down a long tunnel. He could see a dimly lit hall and heard the angry buzz of dozens of men who stood between the stone columns of the great hall. As he entered, Mycroft noticed the high ceilings and huge open window that allowed the full moon to shine its beams into the center of the building. A long veil separated an uplifted stage from what was behind it. It reminded him of a vaudeville hall, with audience facing the podium and curtains in front of them.

As he was ushered to the center of the theater, a drum began to beat and the murmurs of the men crowded into the hall ceased. Quietly at first but growing ever louder, they began to chant, *"Discedite malignus, discedite malignus,"* over and over till the words branded themselves in Mycroft's brain. A ram's horn's shrill blast raked the chant, bringing it to an abrupt stop. It was not the melodious bass timbre Mycroft had heard while visiting

Palestine but a shrieking nasal bleat like a goat dying of congestion. Deathly quiet wrapped its cold tentacles around his heart and squeezed.

Mycroft thought he could hear whimpers but wasn't sure. His attention was quickly drawn to the stage as the headmaster stepped down from the podium and stood before him. He motioned to two men who grabbed hidden chains and manacled Mycroft, who gasped and lunged against his chains. The headmaster pointed to the dark veil, and it parted. In front of him stood four crosses, and chained to them were Holmes' friends, Francis and Jonnie Alparts, Marie Armont, and John Watson. Their clothes were tattered, and blood dripped from several wounds.

Mycroft was stunned. He looked openmouthed at the headmaster whose wicked, arrogant laugh filled the hall. "Oh, Mycroft, you thought to deceive us, to attack us, to use your brother's sacrifice to lull us and expose us to your treachery. But we caught you. We expected deceit and you did not disappoint us. And now you pay for your treason. What you intended for our evil, our god has turned to victory." The man pulled back his hood, stepped out of his robe, and stood naked as the day he was born. He had a long sword in his hand and drew it above his head. Then right as it reached its full height and he was about to plunge it into Mycroft, he shouted, "And now you pay!"

Light flashed from the balcony, a loud shot rang, and a bright red hole appeared in the man's forehead. His eyes crossed and a horrible look of disappointment traversed his face. A dozen other shots rang like a sudden hailstorm on a metal roof from the entrances of the hall. Francis Alparts twisted his wrists and his manacles fell like old newspaper. Jonnie did the same with a similar result. Marie simply moved her arms and the manacles melted away like butter. Jonnie turned and ripped the chains from Watson, but not before her husband in all his savagery roared, jumping into the panicked crowd. From the moonlit window ceiling, glass shattered and ropes fell onto the warehouse floor as men in dark uniformed clothes slid down, strafing the panicked crowd with shotgun blasts. The crimson-robed demon worshipers screamed as they realized the doors were bolted and they were locked in with monsters.

When the smoke had settled and the bodies were covered and what few were allowed to surrender had, a tall, lean figure, with a scar running from above his right eye across his forehead to below the right side of his jaw, walked up to Marie Armont and said, "Now aren't you glad you chose to side with us?"

Her eyes brightened, but her lips wouldn't admit to it and scowled. "Thomas Spurgeon, you did not give me a choice. And besides that, I still don't know who you are and whose side you're on."

He gazed down at her small frame. "Not so very long ago, our nation tolerated slavery in our colonies. Philanthropists endeavored to destroy slavery, but they could not. Politicians railed against it, but their words landed on deaf ears. Do you know when it was utterly abolished? It was when Wilberforce, a sickly, dying man, fell on his face crying out to the Almighty and roused the church of God. And when the bride rose and took to battle, embracing the conflict, she tore the evil thing to pieces. What most people do not know is on the day after England outlawed slavery and three days before he died, Wilberforce turned to a friend and asked with laughter in his heart, 'Is there not something else we can abolish?' That was said playfully, but it shows the spirit of the church of God. She lives in conflict and victory; her mission is to destroy everything that is bad in the land."

"That is not the church I know!"

"Then you do not know the church! But only a paltry shadow of what should be, a vaccination against what ought to be. You know weak-kneed clergy and congregants who don't know a psalm from a gospel, and have never had their hearts broken over their selfishness or their addictive self-indulgence. Neither do you know the one whose trumpet blast will split the skies and join at last with His pure and spotless bride." He halted his torrent of words and leaned over Marie, staring intently into her wide eyes.

"But you caught a glimpse of her today; she pulled back the veil for a quick moment and you saw the dark hordes of this place run. Now you know who we are." He looked down at her again, his feelings hidden behind the hard mask of a warrior. "What do you think? Are you with us?"

Marie tilted her head and stared into his grey eyes. "You know... Thomas, I think... I have been for a very long time."

The next day in the Strangers' Room of the Diogenes Club

Jonnie Alparts looked across to her new best friend, Marie Armont, and whispered in a voice that would have rivaled the master of ceremonies at the annual convention of the deaf, "I thought they didn't allow women in the Diogenes Club?"

"I don't believe either of the Mr. Holmeses asked. And since our presence is by invitation, and Mycroft is a founding member and there seems to have been a sudden and unexplainable drop in membership, especially senior members, the rules have been suspended... or so I hear," Marie replied, trying not to gloat but failing miserably.

Jonnie's husband, Francis, still sore and irritable from a dozen wounds, growled, "Be that as it may, ladies, I am quite confident that suspension might suddenly be revoked if you don't adhere to the primary rule of this house!"

"What rule?" they chimed in deceitful chorus.

Francis scowled suspiciously, glaring at the beautiful eyes innocently flashing back at him. "The keep-your-mouth-shut rule!" he grumbled. But his admonition must have worked because they turned their backs on him and huddled their heads together, whispering so low he could barely hear them.

Mycroft waddled into the room, smoking like the stack on a tramp steamer. "Ladies, I am honored by your presence." He bowed, which was more difficult for him than most people, and began, "I have invited you here today, with your husband and Dr. Watson, who was exasperatingly called away due to an irreconcilable situation he felt compelled to attend." He sighed deeply, rolling his eyes. "Even though it pains me considerably, mention must be made of my sibling, who in spite of his insidious malfeasance had some slight role in the events you starred in so admirably."

Mycroft's penchant for elitism and his anger toward his brother was fully manifest, and Jonnie Alparts was having a difficult time heeding the primary rule of the house. Francis gently grabbed her hand and squeezed. She was about to stare a hole into him when she felt her other hand also grabbed, but by the petite digits of Marie Armont. So, she bit her lip and continued to gaze straight ahead.

Mycroft plodded on, unruffled, in a very formal tone, "Because of the sensitive nature of your achievement, and the ongoing nature of the investigation, I apologize for the clandestine nature of this ceremony." At the word *ceremony*, everyone perked up. A man dressed in the uniform of a British general stepped into the room. He held a silver tray and; on it lay three small black velvet boxes. Mycroft continued, "Francis Alparts, Jonnie Alparts, and Marie Armont, it is my pleasure to present to you the highest award the empire can bestow on one of its subjects, the Victoria Cross."

The same time at 221B Baker Street

"No! Absolutely not! I forbid it." Red-faced John Watson's angry cry reached through the walls and down the stairway to the kitchen. Mrs. Hudson smiled and shook her head. They were at it again like to old widder women fussing and a'fighting.

"But, Watson, just think..."

"You are daft, man. Absolutely daft... And nothing you can say is going to make me agree with you on this."

"I do pay half the rent on this apartment, Watson..." Holmes argued.

"And you will be paying all of it if you follow through on this insanity. It's not right, I tell you, especially now that the Alpartses and Marie spend a good quantity of time here. It is simply not appropriate, Holmes, and a gentleman would not even consider such a thing."

"Gentlemen do it all the time, Watson. Surely you have seen their trophies, framed in eternal glory..." The twinkle in Holmes' eye gave him away. John Watson knew his friend and had been trained by his friend, and when the smile hiding behind Holmes' eyes peered out, Watson caught him.

"Now I see it! You are mocking me, horribly. You are a wicked man, Sherlock Holmes! I left the Diogenes Club, rushed here to stop you from this atrocity, and now I see it... you tricked me."

"So, you don't think I should mount it over the mantel?"

"No, Holmes. It's not even yours. I mean it is but it isn't; you have it on loan and it needs to be returned posthaste to Madame Tussaud's."

"Well, you're a crotchety beggar." Holmes laughed, pulling his wax head out of the box sitting on the floor. He positioned it over the fireplace mantel, then looked back to Watson for approval. Shaking his head, Watson sneered and went back to reading the paper. "Perhaps just bring it out for Christmas or at least until the Alpartses come back from the Diogenes Club."

Watson huffed and did not bother to reply.

Diamonds

"Happy birthday to you, happy birthday to you, happy birthday, dear Bob, happy birthday to you!"

Bob Alparts was growing like a bad weed, or at least that is what his uncle John Watson said as he grabbed Bob by the hands and raised him up and down to the floor. He passed him to Thomas Spurgeon, whose turn it was to "bump" the child, and of course Spurgeon added a blessing to his part of the celebration.

As he lifted the boy in the air, he said, "Arise, O child. May God's might uphold you and His word speak to you, and His hand guard you and His shield protect you. May His hosts save you whether afar or near, alone or in a multitude."

Then it was Marie's turn to "bump" the boy. She had been thinking about what to say. Bumping was a tradition where family and friends tossed the child in the air one time for each year, two for luck, and three for the old man's coconut, whatever that foolishness meant. She knew the power of words and that the blessing of family carried weight, so even though the blessing was for the child, his parents were listening. She grabbed the boy, who was pretty hefty for a three-year-old—but considering who his parents were, the child did not have a genetic chance of being small—and lifted him squealing into the air. "May the love of God and the fear of Him grow in you from your youth, so that by the power of God you will keep the faith. May you vow by God to teach the heathen, though you be despised by some."

The eyes of Jonnie Alparts, the literal bride of the Frankenstein monster, glistened as she heard her best friend bless Bob. Jonnie knew the struggle Marie had had with the leadership of the traditional church. Marie's gifts had closed doors to her and brought persecution, till Thomas Spurgeon had wrapped his cloak around her like Boaz of old. Jonnie's thoughts were snatched back from her meditations by the squawk of her other child: Deborah, born six months earlier and still nursing, and like her mother prone to making her opinions known.

Seeing Jonnie hauling Deborah on one hip while trying to cut birthday cake, Marie said, "Here, hand me that baby."

Jonnie jumped at the opportunity and handed the child to her friend, then loudly pronounced to the rest of the extended family, "It's time to cut the cake. Anyone have any words?"

Holmes grumbled, "Just one. I don't want the thimble. Every time I attend one of these gatherings, I wind up with the bloody thimble, and so far, the curse has borne out."

Watson snorted, almost losing his squash, a lemon-flavored drink traditionally served at children's birthday parties, out his nose. "Holmes, you know you have never had time or inclination to pursue the fairer sex. Why grumble now?"

"Observation, old friend: you, Francis, and now perhaps even Thomas Spurgeon." Holmes motioned with his own glass of squash toward Thomas, whose eyes feasted on

Marie as she cared for little Deborah. "It all brings on a bit of melancholy."

Watson nodded, but they were interrupted by a knock and a yell from the front door by Mrs. Hudson. "Mr. Holmes, you have a visitor."

Marie whispered, "That's what we get for leaving the apartment door open. Some nefarious crime has befuddled the local constabulary and they have found their way to this door again..."

Thomas Spurgeon shrugged. "Marie, you know better than anyone here, *'Ils doivent envisager qu'une grande responsabilité est la suite inséparable d'un grand pouvoir.'* With great power comes great responsibility."

"Yes, dear Thomas, but do you know, my love, that the very people you just quoted are the ones who executed thousands of innocents during the revolution?"

"I wasn't aware, but I am not surprised. Humanity is noted for violating its own conscience time and time again."

Their conversation was interrupted by Jonnie putting her finger to her lips and turning to face the door. Francis cocked his head, quiet and tense. "I hear jingling spurs," Jonnie whispered. Everyone hushed. The only voice in Holmes' apartment was Deborah's, and even she realized something was amiss.

A quick knock rapped on the door. Francis approached and opened it, deliberately stiffening, and preparing for whatever answered.

An officer of the queen's household cavalry regiment stood in full uniform at the door. The man was a hair over six feet, and Holmes could tell he was the captain by the ornamental braided shoulder cord known as an aiguillette. This particular cord was gilded with gemstone points. A high-ranking officer indeed. He wore a gold helmet adorned with a long horsehair plume; his chest armor was a metal cuirass. He was tasked with delivering special messages from the queen.

He took one look at Francis and his hand moved to his sword, but then he saw Thomas Spurgeon and relaxed.

Thomas Spurgeon stiffened almost to attention, old habits dying hard. He made eye contact with the guard captain, who acknowledged him with a slight nod.

"I am sorry to interrupt, Mr. Holmes, but you are needed immediately. The queen sends her regards and apologies for interrupting your day but asks if you would come posthaste to her assistance. I am obliged to escort you, sir."

Holmes nodded to the captain, then turned to his friends and extended family. "I will return as soon as I can." He looked at the guard captain. "Am I allowed to bring an assistant?"

"You are so long as they are essential to an investigation. Her Majesty has already called for and been advised by Scotland Yard, and it was those detectives who advised her to summon you, sir."

"I see, and may I ask—this might be pertinent to the investigation—the nature of the incident?"

"Yes, sir. I have been ordered to share whatever information you might need."

"So, Captain, what happened?"

"The Cullinan Diamond was stolen, sir. The corner piece of the crown jewels has gone missing from its case."

Snow could have fallen and made more noise than Holmes and his companions. The only sounds were Bob slurping on his squash and Deborah cooing.

Then John Watson whistled. "Merciful heavens! How could that be? London Tower is guarded by a dozen troops. Those jewels are never out of sight, and they are protected by a large glass case that would have to have been broken. Surely that would have made some noise."

The captain shook his head. "I don't rightly know, sir. That is why Mr. Holmes' presence has been requested. Is there anyone you wish to accompany you, sir?"

Watson had already started to put his jacket on as a matter of course. Holmes stared at the floor a moment, then asked the captain, "You said the Cullinan Diamond was stolen. Was only one jewel taken? Were no others?"

"Just the one, sir."

"Interesting." Holmes looked around the room. "I know all of you would like to come, and I am sure that you would be helpful, but this is Bob's birthday, and his parents do not need to be called away from it. Watson is like my right arm, so I can't do without him, but... I have a sense that this case may involve the use of gifts that neither Watson nor I share. So Marie, would you be so gracious as to accompany us?"

Marie paled, then wanted to squeal and jump up and down but stopped herself. Covering her mouth with her hand, she nodded once and went to get her coat. She looked back at Spurgeon apologetically.

His head dipped in understanding. "Of course," he whispered. She smiled back at her husband with a radiance that caused him to redden and think things he would have to repent of when he got home. Then she was out the door following Holmes and Watson.

The twenty-minute carriage ride from 221B Baker Street had never been made in such style. The queen's own carriage escorted by a half dozen of her cavalry guard swept down the cobblestone streets as every other carriage and cab hastened aside. Holmes was surprised at the ride's smoothness; usually his gums were sore from his teeth knocking about his head on a cab ride. But this was the queen's carriage, so the springs must have been designed by a clockmaker.

That wisp of thought did not abide long because Marie and Watson were hard at a discussion of the history of the Tower of London and the Cullinan Diamond, the largest gem-quality rough diamond ever found. In its present uncut form, it weighed approximately a pound and a half (using western weight) and was as large as an apple. If rumor had it right, it was destined to be cut and polished and placed into the scepter of England.

Watson listened to Marie excitedly babble about the tower and the diamond, explaining tidbits of history, working herself into a state he was tempted to prescribe laudanum for, when she suddenly switched moods, becoming melancholy and delving into the history of the woman who, in 1815, grabbed the crown and tore its arches off, and was later declared insane.

"Wait a minute, my dear... hold on... your lips are moving faster than my old ears can hear, and my brain has backtracked and then completely derailed. So, pause. Just pause." He put his hands up in front of her, and she stopped her chatter. "I am intrigued by the detail you bring to the conversation, but there is a question nagging at the back of my exhausted brain, and it will not leave me be. So, I must ask. How do you know these things? You have shared that twenty-two guards are stationed around the jewels and that thirty-eight yeomen actually live on-site, and you even know the thickness of the plate glass that surrounds the jewels. How... How?" His brow furrowed as he considered whom he was talking to and speculated on why she would know these details. "Why do you know?"

It was just Marie and Holmes and Dr. Watson in the carriage, but even so she bent over and whispered, "Because, dear doctor, I was charged with robbing them a decade or so back. Then the Masters decided it was easier to take over the government and own the jewels outright rather than steal them. So, the mission was canceled."

Holmes' eyebrows rose to the top of his head and remained firmly seated. Watson gasped like a minnow out of water. Finally, he shook himself and regained the ability to breathe, then shuddered again and turned to look out the window.

But Holmes took up the lecture. "The diamond was discovered at the Premier Number Two Mine in South Africa. It was named after Thomas Cullinan, the mine's chairman. Shortly after its discovery, it was put on sale in England but, despite significant interest, remained unsold after two years. Then it was presented to the monarch by the Transvaal Colony, where it now waits to be cut."

The carriage rolled to a stop outside the walls of the Tower of London, ending the conversation. The captain opened the carriage door, took Marie's proffered hand, and helped her down. Holmes and Watson, left to themselves, quickly vacated the carriage. They were escorted through the thick walls, and even though they all knew the intimidating nature of the fortress, it made an impression, which William the Conqueror had intended when he built it in 1066. Once they entered one of the great halls and looked down the history-filled corridors, they saw the formally uniformed guards. And then... Marie started to see the others.

Two boys, ages twelve and ten, ran down the hall, their ghostly footsteps clattering against the walls. The guards could not hear them, but Marie followed them. They stopped when they noticed her watching them. Their icy stares caused a cold ripple to run the length of her spine. They were dressed in over-gowns with full upper sleeves intended to broaden their shoulders, snug jackets, and breeches that ended in hose for greater comfort. Their shirts were embroidered in black silk with small frills at the neck. Their garments and their manner were formal. Remembering her research, Marie knew who they were: the sons of Edward IV who had vanished within the tower's walls.

The ghosts drew near her but didn't stop her or communicate, so she continued with Holmes and Watson down the cold stone corridor. But now she had been noticed and other pale figures joined her. A slender woman, obviously a queen, was escorted by a roguish man with a twinkle in his eye and a muddy cape. Two other women, and a man who could have been taken off the streets the day before, German by appearance, spy by vocation, watched as they walked by. They fell in behind her as she entered the crown jewels room.

Scotland Yard's best detective, Grayson Lestrade, greeted Holmes. "Very glad to see you, sir." The short, wiry man with bulldog jowls and matching tenacity clasped hands with Holmes and Watson, vigorously greeting them, then bowed to Marie. Lestrade was a regular guest at Holmes' apartment and had met all his associates. He wasn't privy to their backstories but had come to know them as individuals and eventually friends to share a gin and a game of whist. He had endured Jonnie's teasing and recently enjoyed listening to Marie's tales of history—that she had researched from scholarly journals, of course.

Holmes jumped right to it. "Tell me, Grayson, what's happened here?"

"High points first, sir?" He flipped his police pad open, took the short pencil he normally carried in his coat pocket, and checked off items as he shared them with Holmes.

Marie listened intently, then felt a chill and a hand on her shoulder. She started, drawing Lestrade's and Holmes' attention, then stuttered and blurted, "Apologies; someone walked over my grave."

Lestrade smiled and nodded. "This is certainly the place where that could happen. People claim to have seen ghosts here."

He turned his attention back to Holmes, who wondered why the only person in the room who could see the dead referred to a grave being walked on. He filed the thought, intent on taking it up with Marie at a more appropriate occasion.

Watson leaned into her and whispered, "Your grave or someone else's?"

Marie's only answer was the microscopic raising of an eyebrow and then easing away from Holmes and Lestrade's conversation. The room was filled with people, some of whom were alive. The bobbies and Scotland Yard's detectives, of course, were among those with a pulse, but some of the guards and all of the elegantly clad ladies were not.

Marie turned to see who had touched her. A woman who must have died in her late teens stared back at her with deep-set brown eyes beneath a high forehead. Her hair was red gold; she was almost six feet tall and light and graceful with long white fingers. A thin line circled her neck, the mark of the axe man. "I know why you are here," she said in a whisper as ghostly as her body. "We saw who took the diamond."

Marie blanched. Her mouth opened quickly and then just as quickly shut. She couldn't speak aloud, but the woman understood and continued, "Nod if you want to know more." She motioned toward the others and back to Marie. "Do you think you can slip away and speak with us? We would like to help but understand you have to be careful."

Marie nodded and then beneath her breath replied, "I'll find a way." She edged closer to Watson, who had been listening to Holmes questioning Lestrade. "Dr. Watson, I am feeling indisposed. I'm going to find a retiring room and freshen up."

Watson knew better but responded, "I understand. Take your time." And then in a whisper meant only for her, "You will probably come back with more answers than we get here."

A demure smile answered him, and she moved away and down the hall. She entered a side room that had been furnished with toilets and discovered that ghosts had little sense of personal space. They crowded the room, standing and hovering all the way to the ceiling. Their presence chilled her so that her breath came in a fleeting misty cloud. She wrapped her shawl tightly around her and began, "I still need to keep my voice down. I am grateful for your help. Now please share with me what you saw."

The tall, extravagantly dressed man with the roguish air, who looked like a combination attorney pirate, spoke. "I think I speak for all of us when I say it is a pleasure to address one of the living again."

Marie nodded and waited. She could tell the man was just getting warmed up.

"We would like to help you. Lady Jane was there when the deed was done and saw the fairy that took the bauble."

Marie perked up; she wasn't expecting to hear the word *fairy*.

"I see that surprises you, madam. It did us as well. She waltzed right into the room, hiding beneath a fairy glamor, the illusion fairies project that hides them from any prying eyes, and cut the glass with her fingernails. Then she reached her arm in, skipped over several jewels, and took the largest gemstone. She left the others behind and waltzed out. We know who she was and where she hails from, but now, before we share that information, we would ask your help..."

Marie tilted her head and rubbed her chin. "Of course I will do all I can. But what help can I offer you?"

One of the women, a young woman possibly seventeen, stepped forward. "We are stuck here, some of us because of our sins, others of us for reasons we do not know. But in the time we have been here, we have all come to realize that trouble comes because it is invited. And often the consequences are visited upon the innocent simply because they were in the wrong place at the wrong time or believed the wrong people."

Many of those gathered nodded, and a few of them echoed, "Hear, hear!"

The young woman continued, "All that to say, in the past our nation has done many evil things, some from ignorance or out of fear, but most simply from greed or covetousness. And to make a long story short, we saw who took the great diamond, but what confuses us is what they didn't take, and why. I am sure from listening to the bobbies' chatter that they suffer the same confusion."

Marie's face gave away her surprise. "Well... this certainly puts things in a new light. I don't know how it will change the investigation, but hmmm... I will have to take this up with Mr. Holmes. But I will not share it with the people who don't believe that fairies steal or ghosts witness crime. Goodness, I was not expecting this. And thank you... is that what you wished of me? To convey this message and see how the investigation changes in light of it?"

"Not totally," the young woman replied. "Some of us, or our bodies at least, were interned under wrongful duress. They just wanted to get rid of us, and the location of old bones shouldn't be a problem. But for some reason it is, because instead of moving on, a part of us remains. We do not understand why unless..." A hush colder than snow on tombstones and quieter still settled on the ghosts gathered in the small room. It was a collective sigh, an acknowledgment of guilt and a sorrow that had lasted so long the walls dripped with it and the living could sense it when they walked the halls. She ended the pause and continued, "It is part of our punishment. Whatever the case, would you, as much as lies within you, look into this and help us? We are so weary of this ancient rock prison and would desperately like to move on."

Marie's head was nodding, reflecting her heart's decision already made to help these people as best she could. "Yes, of course. I will certainly."

"We thought you would, so here is what we know. She was royalty, possibly even a queen of the fairies."

Marie looked around the room. The history of England stood before her, its triumph and mostly its tragedy arrayed in their eternal glory. "I will do my best to help you. Somehow, some way. I will see this through. Don't despair."

Then one by one the phantoms vanished, ending with the roguish face of the tall man she guessed had to be Sir Walter Raleigh, who smiled and then winked and was gone.

Marie opened the door to the ladies' restroom right as Dr. Watson was poised to knock. Red-faced, he let out a great breath when she appeared before him. He took one look at her and whispered, "I can see your investigation has been more fruitful than ours, but I am afraid that Holmes has to go through the expected procedurals, even though I can tell he has concluded the thief is not an ordinary individual. Can you give me the highlights? We can take a walk down these drafty halls while Holmes goes through the motions. I have a feeling your story will be absolutely mind-boggling."

The Long Game

Three hours later, back at 221B Baker Street

Marie stuffed the last piece of Bob's birthday cake in her mouth and chewed slowly, savoring every delightful morsel. Mrs. Hudson was an amazing baker and the cake was spectacular. It was called a Battenburg cake, a light sponge cake held together with jam and covered in marzipan, a confection consisting primarily of honey and almond meal. But the most impressive thing about the cake was its alternately colored checkered patterns of pink and yellow. Marie groaned with every mouthful.

Watson grabbed his stomach, complaining he had eaten too much while stuffing his face with another morsel. He chomped down on the coin hidden inside the cake and yelled, "What the bloody?" then realized he had just been blessed with good fortune, being the individual to find the coin in the cake.

Holmes, on the other hand, stared at the thimble on his finger that he had discovered in his slice. "I should have known, fated to be sure. But probably for the best..." He didn't want to believe that but had about convinced himself it must be true.

Francis and Jonnie were holding hands, while Spurgeon diligently searched an old manuscript between bites of the birthday cake. He was surprised to find in Holmes' library an ancient Christian text, specifically, the collected writings of the church fathers on supernatural creatures. "Sherlock, where on earth did you find such a book? This is amazing."

Holmes motioned for the manuscript, opened it to the title page, and handed it back to Spurgeon. The inscription read, *To my dear Detective Holmes, I pray as heaven's doors have cracked and given you a glimpse, so the pages of this old book will also enlighten you. I have a sense you are going to need it, especially now as the door is open. Your humble servant, Monsignor Henri*

Spurgeon was a scholar by nature, and when he read the inscription he nodded and asked, "So what do you think about the testimony Marie gathered from the specters that haunt the tower?"

"I think it is good that we have passports. The problem is going to be how we convince Scotland Yard to pay for our trip to South Africa. We can't tell them we are headed there because a room full of ancient queens and pirates witnessed the theft, now can we?"

Francis savored his last bite of Battenburg birthday cake. "You know, fellows, even though a fairy may have stolen the jewel, it seems to me that she still suffers the same constraints as a human."

Sherlock cocked his head and stared at his massive friend. "How so, Francis?"

"Either they will try to get the stone out of the country or they have a buyer they are trying to get it to. Surely no one who could steal it out from under the noses of twenty-two guards would do so without a means of disposing of the gem."

Holmes grunted, and every eye in the room turned on Francis, who was totally in his own world focusing on the next logical steps the thief would have to take.

"So, if you change your focus from how he did it to what he has to do with it, well, who knows, it may turn something up?"

Spurgeon ran his finger down a yellowed page toward the back of the manuscript he studied. He found what he was looking for and flipped back into the book. Finding a certain page, he read silently and then a huge smile lit his features. "My friends, I had an impression and I followed it, and look where it led. Marie, confirm for me, please, that the ghost told you the creature was a fairy, possibly royalty?"

"Yes, Thomas, that is what they said."

Spurgeon began to read. "'Fairies are hoarders. They love gold and fine jewels, and like dragons, they keep their valuables in piles and chests, and determine their significance by the size of their hoards.' I don't think our thief is going to sell this gem. I think she is going to find a place, or already has a place, she intends to keep it. I don't know if that helps or not?"

"It definitely narrows the parameters of the search. Scotland Yard will be looking for a human with human motivations and habits, but we shall be searching elsewhere," Holmes added.

Francis opened his mouth to comment when his preternatural hearing kicked in. He cocked his head and listened. Jonnie saw him and immediately quieted. That infrequent behavior caused everyone else to hush and watch what the couple was about.

Francis whispered, "The front door opened and someone is sneaking up the stairs."

Spurgeon moved silently and swiftly toward the door. Jonnie stood between her sleeping children and the door, Holmes pulled his revolver, and Francis backed up Spurgeon with his massive frame and a claymore sword that fit him like a regular sword would a normal-size man. Marie stood next to Jonnie, and they waited. If whoever was about to walk through that door meant evil, they had an extremely unpleasant surprise waiting.

There was a long awkward pause. Jonnie whispered to Marie, "I can hear a heartbeat behind the door. Male, late thirties, athletic, smoker, curious as to why we stopped talking."

Holmes reached for the knob, nodded to Spurgeon, and yanked the door open. No one was standing there.

The collective gasp sucked the air out of the room. Then there was the rattle of a dozen questions, and then everyone else joined Jonnie with their own questions.

Holmes stared, then grasped Spurgeon by one hand and Francis by the other, creating a human wall around the door. "Quiet! We do have a guest, just not a visible one."

Francis drew in a quick breath. "I smell him, chemicals, and bandages."

Marie barked out, "To your left, gentlemen, standing outside the door, leaning against the rail."

Holmes nodded and faced the general direction that Marie had indicated. "Good evening, Jack Griffin. If you intend us well, you are welcome. If not, then prepare to deal with the deadliest community in the empire."

A voice, Scottish by the brogue, answered, "I don't mean you harm, Mr. Holmes, but I did think it prudent to scout you out before knocking on your door. But it appears to me your own scouts are extremely sophisticated. You have it on my honor, sir, that I am here to parley and have no dishonorable intentions."

"That is very wise of you, sir, since two of our company would discern immediately if you did, and then two more would dissuade you violently if need be of those intentions, and then of course one of us would be available to stitch you up after said dissuasion... so, based on your word, come in, for you are welcome."

Spurgeon and Francis dropped back. They felt a figure pass, and then Marie said, "Mr. Griffin, please be so gracious as to sit in one of Mr. Holmes' wooden chairs, but first let me place a towel in the chair of your choice, sir."

Jack Griffin laughed. "Cleanliness is next to godliness, fair lady." Then they all watched wide-eyed as a chair beneath the table moved of its own accord, flew slowly through the air, and seated itself in the semicircle made by the rest of Holmes' den furniture. "Will this do, ma'am?" Marie nodded and offered a bath towel toward the voice. Something grabbed it and draped it over the chair's wooden seat.

Francis' puzzled look caused Marie to answer the unasked question. "Invisibility does not include his garments." Francis shivered as the thought took hold.

"Aye, and it is a bit chilly out tonight, guvnor, but I have gotten used to it over the years. Although if you would be gracious to offer a shawl or something of the sort, my teeth might not rattle as hard."

Jonnie went for a blanket while Marie looked in the direction of the invisible man and handed him another bath towel. He laughed and said, "You are a very tidy lady, I will say that for you." The second towel draped over an invisible lap, and then the blanket wrapped itself around an unseen frame. Holmes reached up to his own garment rack and offered the deerstalker cap to an invisible hand, then watched as it found its way onto an unseen head.

"That will help us converse with you, sir. Thank you for your tolerance of our unfamiliarity with your circumstances."

Jack Griffin crossed his legs but no one noticed. Holmes had a very enlightening moment as he sat in front of a man he could not visually scrutinize. He suddenly understood what it was like to be blind and how much he depended on his sight to guide his evaluations. It set him back and for a moment left him speechless. His associates, accustomed to his typical astounding revelations of client circumstances, realized their chief was struggling. So it was that the conversation began with an insight from the least likely of the friends.

Francis looked in the general direction of their indistinguishable guest and said, "Sir, my sense of smell is finely developed, and I can sense that you are anxious, but not particularly fearful—more aggravated than afraid. You have also recently been wounded rather deeply, probably from a knife or dagger, so you have been in a fight."

A grunt from under the deerstalker cap gave credence to the giant man's olfactory ability. But before he could confirm it, another voice from an unexpected quarter spoke up. Marie added, "And I have the ability to see beyond veils, to pick up residue of powerful emotional encounters. And therefore, I agree with Francis that you are agitated and it is because of the violence you were recently involved in."

"Seriously, mate, I'm in a room full of seers and mediums. Feel almost naked I do, but what else? This is fun." A highly entertained invisible man laughed.

Once again someone relatively new to Holmes' procedures, but also extremely gifted as an investigator, added his insight. "Mr. Griffin, you have a history of thievery. Some of the most amazing and unsolved thefts of the last ten years have been laid at your door. Especially jewel thefts. But that is not the case in the most recent theft of the Cullinan Diamond; yet you are here. So therefore you are involved with its disappearance in some manner, and since you would probably not have darkened our door"—Spurgeon paused as eyeballs rolled on his last remark, with Jonnie's and Watson's being the most dramatic—"had you been the one to steal the diamond, you must somehow be at odds with the person who used powers similar to yours and hid behind invisibility to steal it."

"Jiminy, guvnor, you let these people keep this up and you are gonna be out of work! They are good, but we have not heard from the master. What say ye, Mr. Sherlock Holmes, now that your apprentices have plowed a righteous furrow and shown the way? What do you surmise, sir?"

"They are superb, are they not?" Holmes beamed like the proud professor he was. "They have given me perspicacity and direction using their amazing gifts and insight that I didn't have access to previously. But let me see if I can build on them.

"You are at odds with the fairy who stole the diamond because they did not take it to profit from the theft but to restore it to the original owner. After you heard of the theft, you hunted them down, knowing who they were and how to reach them because you were the one who stole from them originally. But you met with violence and then realized you needed help to get the gem back. So, you came to us thinking you could persuade us to help you take back the diamond because it belonged to the empire. When, truthfully, it does not. So, we must disappoint you, sir, because now we realize it was stolen property to begin with, and you stole it for the Cullinan Mining Company, who then sold it to the unwitting"—Holmes paused as a hard question occurred to him: *Was that true, did they really not know?* — "British government. Who I am certain, when they discover the gem is stolen property, will insist on its return to its rightful owner?"

"Ah, but you missed it, Mr. Holmes. You see, I am not here on my own recognizance, not at all, sir. I am here as the dutiful and, truth be told, probationary representative of the British government. They hired me to get it back, one way or the other. Takes an invisible thief to catch an invisible thief, if you will, sir. And I thought while I was about it that I might just take up with you, and we could combine our insights and efforts and resources—if you catch my meaning, sir, 'cause you have some formidable folks here—and steal the property back for its original... I was going to say *owners*, but perhaps a better word might be more appropriate? Possessors, holders, maybe even... thieves, if ya will."

For the second time in a few moments Sherlock Holmes was speechless.

Every eye in the room not staring at the deerstalker cap—and that was all of them except Holmes—was riveted on Sherlock's face, waiting for his response.

He took a deep breath. "Mr. Griffin, all we have at the moment is your word that you have been rightfully commissioned by Her Majesty's government to... acquire the Cullinan Diamond. And you have to admit, sir, that is a lot to ask on faith, considering your previous... accounts." Holmes was reaching and everyone in the room knew it. He was throwing up plausible concerns in order to buy time, to think through his options. Jack Griffin knew it also. His face was not visible, but his contempt was discernable. Rising temperature, shortness of breath, squeaky chair, all shouted that the guest, although invisible, was definitely offended.

"So that's how it is? Well, you know that I will never have a paper commissioning me to steal the diamond. That is just not what old frumpy, lumpy, stern, and grumpy Miss We-are-not-amused would ever risk putting on paper, sir. Her friends, or at least the people whose opinions matter to her—I don't think her kind ever have what a normal person would call friends—would be appalled to know the empire was little more than an unscrupulous pawnbroker, just dealing in better stock. So, I don't have any proof. But you do not know the whereabouts of the current thief, sir. So you have something I need, and I have something..."

"On the contrary, Mr. Griffin, we do know the whereabouts, or can in short order, so your services are not required."

A palpable chill swept through the den. Griffin rose, the towels and blanket tumbled off him, and the chair fell backwards. "Don't turn your back, Mr. Holmes, and that goes for all of you. But it doesn't really matter, does it, whether your back is turned or not because..." He jumped toward Marie, who was standing next to Thomas, his hand a hidden serpent striking an unaware victim.

But he had underestimated Thomas Spurgeon, who practiced physical combat blindfolded and, combined with his own lightning speed and keenly honed intuition, caught Griffin's fist in mid-strike, turned it, and had the man flailing on the floor in a heartbeat. Francis joined Thomas, placing his massive knee in the unseen assailant's back. Griffin huffed as the air was pressed from him, then, gasping, railed on them, "You may have caught me this time, Holmes—you and your freaks—but you won't know when I will strike again, when hidden, lurking like a shadow, I will."

Jonnie Alparts bent low and inhaled deeply, and her husband did the same. Marie's eyes unfocused and blinked a few times and then refocused.

"Mr. Griffin," Holmes began, "your threats are idle. Now let me explain to you why. Your scent, no matter how you might try to disguise it, is forever filed with the Alpartses' amazing sense of smell. They can identify people, even invisible people, simply by their scent. And then as a double safety measure, Marie has looked into the spirit world and seen your aura. You may hide your body, sir, but you cannot hide your soul, and she has the make of it. So, if I were you, I would not come round, not at all, because the moment the wind shifts or your darkened aura breaches the boundaries—and I have it on very excellent authority that can be sensed for up to a mile—we will have you, sir. You have been warned. Now leave!"

An hour later, Jonnie Alparts had her naked feet in her husband's lap. His head was tilted back, his mouth agape. Sleep had overcome them. Marie and Thomas Spurgeon had seen their way out, and Watson had waddled off home to bed. Holmes was seated in his overstuffed chair, puffing on a blackened, disreputable clay pipe more nicked than not. He was well into a three-pipe problem, and the dense, foul clouds of bluish smoke curled around his head like the dragon breath of Smaug, a wyrme from ancient lore.

Jonnie had finally convinced him to purchase a Schuyler Wheeler motorized fan powered by electricity. She had to threaten him by saying she and her brood would never leave him to himself if, when they were in his home, he didn't push his nasty smoke out the window and not up her children's delicate noses. Watson had heartily seconded the motion, and now Holmes couldn't remember life without the amazing device.

But even beneath its warm breeze and his pipe's odorous fumes, Holmes had found nothing that could help him navigate the maze that presented itself. He despised the thought of stealing from the diamond's rightful owners. But what choice did he have? His thoughts blurred with weariness. He could force himself to sort and cull scenarios all night and had done so on many occasions, but now his eyelids were beyond his ability to control and heaved down like the last call of theatre curtains on London's West End.

"Finally! I have never seen such a stubborn man. You are definitely more grit and gristle than you look. But now that you have lowered the threshold, we need to talk."

Holmes' eyes shot open as he bolted awake. In Watson's chair opposite him sat a beautiful woman. She had snow-white curly hair that dangled in long tresses, dark-green eyes, and a golden complexion. She was slender until she wasn't.

And those curves caused even a famed misogynist of Holmes' stripe to take notice.

Sherlock Holmes had never shown any particular interest in women. His stated reason was that love was an emotion that clouds the mind and a clear logical mind was absolutely indispensable to solving crime. A newspaper had described him to be as inhuman as a calculating machine, and he had grown to take pride in identifying with the fine-tuned gears of cold and methodical rationality. And besides that, women were unfathomable, inscrutable, unpredictable, and capable of horrific acts that would make even the London Ripper pause. Or so Holmes liked to say. But the truth, known only to him and hidden so deep that he often forgot where it lay, was that Sherlock Holmes was shy.

He smirked, then said, "I didn't know if we would have to hunt you down or not. I half expected you to present your case and am grateful that you have chosen to do so."

A pointed eyebrow was her first response. "Hmm, and what would you like for me to say, Sherlock Holmes? What would change your mind? Your course of action? Are you courageous enough to oppose your queen? Your whole world would tumble and your name be ruined if you were to side with my cause in this occasion. So why should I even waste my breath upon your door?"

Holmes exhaled a puff of smoke and thought about the woman's words and their double edge. At length he gathered up his courage, discovering it embedded as always in his devotion to honesty. "If you did not believe your word could elicit some type of change, if you truly had no hope, then you would not have come. As shrewd a species as you may represent, you are not so audacious as to court disaster by exposing your motivations to me without some vision of justice driving them. So, tell me your story and let me weigh it.

I promise you if it is true, then I will stand with you even if it is as forlorn as a lone English yew before a cyclone."

The woman's gaze never left him... but her essence did, like a mist dispersed by the dawn. Then right before she was completely gone, he heard her voice from far away. "Come find me, Sherlock. Breathe upon my door and you will have your answers." And with that Holmes awoke with the scent of lavender replacing the awful dragon's breath of his harsh tobacco.

Holmes watched as the early-morning sun crept over the tops of the apartments across from 221B Baker Street. The cool breeze caressed his cheek. It had been a long time since he had awoken feeling so refreshed. He heard a rustling and looked over to see Jonnie and Mrs. Hudson bringing breakfast trays into his apartment. He stood, stretched, and realized his typical early-morning collection of soreness from old wounds he termed *vocational hazards* were not manifesting.

Jonnie looked at him and nearly commented, but then tilted her head and stared as if seeing him for the first time.

Holmes paused in mid-stretch. "Jonnie, is there something out of sorts?"

"Sir, you look different, and not just physically. Did you have any strange dreams during the night?"

Holmes gaped. He should have known better. He had spent three years now with beings who had one foot in this world and one in another, so he shouldn't have been at all surprised by Jonnie's question. But he was. Just as he constantly confounded his associates with his uncanny insights into the clients that darkened his door, so they amazed him with theirs.

"As a matter of fact, I did."

"Well, that explains it then." She went back to sitting at the table.

Francis stumbled in from the bedroom, not at all a morning person. His hair was tousled on his square head like a rumpled spinnaker wrapped around a mast. "Explains what, my love?" The huge man bent down to receive his morning coffee and his kiss, then wrinkled his nose and said, "Gag! Fairy lavender. When did you receive a visitor, Mr. Holmes?"

Shaking his head, Holmes walked to the dining table and sat. "Well, I wasn't sure I had till your mutual confirmations this morning. But now that we've laid that to rest, I will try to answer your questions, in the order I perceived them. Yes, yes, and right before I fell asleep. Now I am going to eat my breakfast and read the paper, and as soon as Marie and Spurgeon make their appearance and Watson finishes his hospital rounds, I shall explain what I have discovered and parcel out the day's assignments."

Jonnie Alparts had learned from repeated and fruitless attempts that prying more from Sherlock Holmes when he was inclined to give less was a wasted effort. So she tucked a bib into Deborah's shirt, handed Francis a blueberry scone, turned back to her daughter, shoved a mouthful of freshly mashed applesauce down her baby-birdlike maw, and waited.

She heard the front door open and knew within seconds that her best friend, Marie Armont Spurgeon, was walking up the stairs with her ruggedly handsome husband, Thomas, right behind her. She heard a swat, a laugh, and then a whisper that could have been shouted in the den for all the good it did. "Stop that, Thomas, and you a clergyman's son!"

"And how'd you expect other clergymen's sons to come about without..." Marie opened the door and Thomas' words abruptly stopped. They walked in and saw Francis and Jonnie sporting red faces while trying to wipe scattered blueberry scone particles from the table where Francis' snort had spread them, vainly trying to look like they hadn't heard every word of the staircase exchange.

Holmes, on the other hand, was a refuge of oblivious ignorance, for which the couple was grateful.

When everyone had quit smirking, choking, and threatening slow death over a spit, and Watson had stomped up the stairs complaining about the sickly-sweet smell of lavender, Holmes began. "As you know or have heard"—he cast a quick glance at Jonnie, who had been nonstop filling Marie's ear— "I had a visitor last night. She came to me in a dream, or at least something similar to a dream, and pleaded her innocence. She did not say that she had not stolen the diamond but that it was hers or her people's to recover. And then she said to seek her out. Now to make a long story short, we shall have to break up into two teams, one of which will go back to the tower and try to determine a way to lay the ghosts to rest. The other will come with me to the fairy nest and negotiate with the creature for the diamond. The Spurgeons seem best equipped to deal with the tower residents and the Alpartses with the fairies, and Watson, I have the strange suspicion that your talents for the forensic may best be served by attending the Spurgeons."

An hour later on the carriage ride to the Tower of London...

Thomas Spurgeon cleared his throat and fiddled with his shirt cuffs. His wife noted his struggle and waited for the inevitable question. "Marie, I have a problem."

She looked back at the man she trusted more than her own heart and knew exactly what he was going to say. "I did not seek them out; I have never sought them for guidance. I know ghosts are often not dead people but demons pretending. But... Thomas, what am I to do when they seek me because I can see them?"

Thomas Spurgeon stroked the scar that streamed above his eyes and down his right hairline. "I know, and I've had this conversation with Theodosia, who assures me there is a difference between a spiritist and a person who is sensitive and only wants to help the departed... well... depart! But... I can think of at least a dozen passages where speaking to the dead is expressly forbidden. In no uncertain terms the living are commanded not to seek out the dead for guidance. So, you and I need to be extremely cautious and discerning, lest we be deceived in this occasion."

Watson interrupted Spurgeon. "Thomas, I know I am not a theologian, and to be honest I'm just barely a newly awakened soul, but it appears to me based on your conversation—and Marie's previous experience with these... ah... folks—that interrogating them would not bear fruit because if they knew what was holding them here, they would have long ago dealt with it. And you perceived no sense of that, did you, my dear?"

"That is correct, Dr. Watson. I was wondering that myself. But if we don't ask them questions, how can we determine consensus and look for patterns that connect them all to the tower?"

Thomas sighed. "We are walking where angels fear to tread, and this time very literally. I know we cannot lump every ghost and those that deal with them into the same old bucket—to quote Dickens, more of *gravey than of grave*—as one extreme, or bow and pray to them as divine ancestral beings at the other. And I am extremely aware, as always, the truth is narrow, with wide ditches full of the incautious littering the way." Thomas could tell that the good doctor had jumped ahead of his own steady train of reason, so he nodded and said, "Forgive my lecture, Dr. Watson. What were you thinking?"

"I hate to be the one to suggest this, seeing as I previously stated I am so new to this illumination that my eyes are still blinking from the brightness, but isn't there another text in the good book that goes something like, 'Should not people inquire of their God? Why consult the dead on behalf of the living?'"

Spurgeon nodded in agreement, urging him on.

"My point being, we are not consulting the dead on behalf of the living but..."

Marie somberly finished. "But on the behalf of the dead."

Thomas frowned and closed his eyes. "We have forgotten something else."

Marie looked at her husband, a gentle smile slipping into its accustomed place. "Yes, we have."

He opened his eyes. "Lead us to the throne, my dear. If you will?"

Marie had never prayed before anyone but her husband. She had cursed and screamed and shouted a thousand times, defiling saints and sinners over her long life, but she had never bowed her head and humbled her heart aloud. A dozen accusations assaulted her—unworthiness, ignorance, a half-dozen simple sins that would thwart any request she made—and then Thomas cleared them all aside by saying, "You know you are the apple of His eye, my dear." He closed his eyes and added, "And He is waiting."

Marie sighed, thinking, *Thomas is going to hear about this later.* Then she realized plans of revenge were not advantageous in approaching the Almighty. So, she began slowly at first, stammering to find her way like a blind person in an unfamiliar room. "Almighty—no, that's not... well, it is, but, Lord God... ahh, again right, but not." Finally, she settled on, "Father... Lord"—and then found the key—"Master? Of course. You alone are Master; You alone are sovereign and just and able. Oh, my Lord. And..." In a hushed tone like the fragrance of fresh baked bread, she said, "Friend. We need Your help. And not really us, but those who have been held back from You for ages, who cannot come to You and Your rest. They need Your help. And they asked me, Lord... I didn't seek them out..."

She paused, waiting, listening, then continued whispering, "Yes, I know You know that. You always weigh our hearts and then," she chuckled, "You put Your thumb on the scale and count us righteous. Grant us wisdom, Lord. Your name is wisdom, and You promised You would give it. So, we believe as we enter this place again that You are going with us and that You will set things straight. In Christ's name, amen."

Watson looked up and saw Marie's face glowing. He glanced at Thomas and saw pride in his wife beaming from his eyes. What he didn't see were the tears in his own.

The cab to the tower stopped. Thomas Spurgeon took a deep breath and said, "All right then, this is it. It has been my experience that we can expect a distraction, but if we stay the course, it will turn out better than expected." He exited the cab, followed by Marie and then Watson.

They walked up to the entrance and were met by several guards. One of the guards took their names and went into the tower. A few minutes later he was followed out, not by the expected captain but by a well-dressed man who appeared to be in his late thirties. He wore a dark bowler and had muttonchops. He was not smiling. He approached the three and asked, "Are you Thomas and Marie Spurgeon and Dr. John Watson?"

Watson stepped forward. "We are."

The man continued, "Well then, thank you for saving me the effort of finding you. I arrest you in the name of Queen Victoria on suspicion of aiding and harboring the thief responsible for the theft of the Cullinan Diamond."

******

Holmes and the Alpartses stepped outside his apartment and looked down the street. They noticed two unfamiliar carriages. Holmes raised his hand to wave down a passing cabbie when Francis' shrill whistle caused every horse for a block to whinny and two cabs to come racing toward them.

"Well, I suppose we can mark stealth off our list of possibilities for the day. If those intent on following us had managed to miss our entrance onto the street, I am quite sure they are aware and grateful for the prod," Holmes grumbled.

Francis looked sheepish and helped his wife and Holmes into the cab. Then he boarded, noticing that the unfamiliar cabs hadn't even bothered to hide the fact they intended to follow them. But this was not Sherlock Holmes' first experience being followed by people he did not want following him. He addressed the Alpartses like he was discussing the route to the circus instead of as a means of throwing the pursuers off the trail.

"Before we left the apartment, I made some plans, and in a moment you will see something as near artwork as a London cabbie can produce. It is almost a ballet. If you would observe, please." Holmes reached through the inside window and slipped the driver a coin. The driver smiled and nodded and, as they crossed Gloucester Place Road, he sped up, while another cab waiting for just that move pulled out in front of the men following Holmes and stopped. The screams of the thwarted men scorched the air, but Holmes' cab continued on at a faster clip.

At York Street two cabs just happened to move from resting on the side to right behind Holmes' cab, and again at Knox, and finally Seymour and two other streets, cabs all from the same company and looking exactly alike pulled behind them. Then, when they were forced to stop at the crossroads of Sussex Place, Holmes yanked up a panel in the bottom of the cab and revealed the cobblestone road beneath. He knocked on the inside window, and the cab advanced three feet. An iron manhole cover appeared.

Holmes barked, "Grab it and pull, Francis."

The giant wrenched the cover back. The smiling, dirty face of one of Holmes' street boys popped up and yelled, "Quick, Mr. Holmes!" and then dived back in the hole. Holmes jumped down, followed by Jonnie, who griped the whole way that he could have warned her and she wouldn't have worn a nice dress. Francis squeezed his great shoulders through last of all and pulled the cab panel and the manhole cover back in place. Just as he did, the cabbie whistled and the cab moved on.

The cabs behind it drove off as well, one going one way and the others going another, till the men following Holmes spotted the original cab that they thought held Holmes and company and sped up to catch it. The cabbie continued to the far side of London where, two hours later, he pulled into his berth at the stable. Behind him six men in two cabs poured out and ran to the door, yanking it open. And twice in one day their loud screams and curses ripped the air.

Beneath the streets of London, Holmes was in familiar territory. "I do apologize, Jonnie. I quite forgot how hot, dirty, and wet these tunnels are. Please forgive me."

Jonnie laughed. "Oh, Mr. Holmes, these are dirty holes for sure, but Francis and I spent a large portion of our early married life here and grew to think of them as a home away from home, so to speak." Francis' eyebrows rose so quickly at Jonnie's embellishment they threatened to stick in his hairline. But a single slight move of one of her own eyebrows deflected any more comment and she continued. "Chances are they haven't changed much in the last few decades. We will be happy to act as tour guides, and when this is done and we've all bathed, you can take us to Pagani's restaurant for penance."

"Done, my dear, absolutely done! Now, if you will, we need to get to the Thames Tunnel."

"Been there many times, Mr. Holmes. If you know where to look and who to ask, you can find some of the best shops in London. They don't cater to the wealthy," she continued.

Francis laughed at Jonnie's phrase *cater to the wealthy*. She elbowed him sharply, but he continued, "And there is a very good reason they don't cater to the wealthy. Because the wealthy might recognize some of the objects being sold as belonging to them!"

Holmes laughed at his two companions. "Just the right place, then, for stolen goods and negotiations?"

An hour of humid, smelly travel and two misturns and one long backtrack later, Holmes' feet were sore from breaking in his new boots and Francis and Jonnie weren't speaking. They came to an iron door. Francis looked at Jonnie to confirm it was the right door. She rolled her eyes and nodded, and then he said, "We are here, Mr. Holmes, but after we open this door, I will not know the way."

"Pretty sure you didn't know the way an hour ago, but no. You wouldn't listen to your wife!" Jonnie added without being invited.

Francis ignored his agitated wife. Holmes responded, "This, my dear Alparts, is where your nose and my eyes and, Jonnie, your ability to sense moods and magic comes to play. The fairies are here, or at least the door leading to one of their nests is. I know it lies near a tunnel under the river, and this is the only tunnel I know of under the river, so this is where we start. I expect our previous company will eventually find its way here. They may already be here. So, be extremely wary. We shall have to walk a distance through the market. Midway, somewhere along this major corridor, will be another door, and that will lead us to where we want to go. But to find it? We shall see."

With that he opened the rusty iron door and walked into an underground market that sold everything a normal person could want, and most of what abnormal people did as well.

Holmes was tempted to allow himself distraction. Stepping from the gloom of the sewer tunnels into an underground marketplace traveled by two million people a year was a jolt. They entered a rotunda fifty feet in diameter, laid in blue and white mosaic. The walls were plastered with advertising banners, everything from the Ringling Brothers' circus to taverns, books, and confections. The smell of cooked meat and pastries mixed with the stale rot of trash hidden behind the vending booths littered the air. People were everywhere, pressing, talking, laughing, with the occasional cry of a tired child or an angry pedestrian. And above it all was the loud blast of a huge organ belting out the latest tunes.

"It's a bloody carnival!" Francis shouted, his hands cupping his mouth to be heard over the crowd. Holmes nodded, moving slowly through the mass of people, his eyes scouring every cranny. The world had gathered beneath the filthy waters of the Thames. Everything from Egyptian necromancers to gypsy fortunetellers and dancing monkeys. The only things Holmes did not see were street cops.

The tunnel was controlled by a network of tunnel thieves. Each criminal had his section, and the vendors in that area paid a tax. If the tax grew outrageous, or the vendor was not protected from crime other than the inescapable extortion, he, or she, had the right to join another network. The thief network was efficient and merciless, ruthlessly dealing with interlopers. Thus bobbies were not needed. As the trio slowly walked through the tunnel, they realized the further they got from the entrance, the more daring the wall banners and the more risqué the women working the booths. Soon it became obvious that if they walked any further, they would be strolling down the large corridor of a brothel.

Francis' face was red. Jonnie's was as well, but for a different reason, and her eyes managed to comb the street and walls before her while not missing a glance that poor Francis took.

Then Holmes grabbed them. "Look right in front of us."

The Alpartses caught Holmes' gaze and followed it to a yellowed, ripped, and curled banner glued to the stuccoed wall. It read, *The door to the Beautiful Land. Enter and enjoy. Price: your soul or ten pence, whichever is cheaper.* Beneath the banner was a large wooden double door also plastered with pictures of scantily clad women and the price of ale. But over to the side, hidden by the shadows, was another door surrounded with a garland of evergreen and white flowers.

Holmes went to the smaller door and realized as throngs of people pushed and gawked and pressed against him and the Alpartses that only they could see the door. It was covered by a glamor. "Interesting..." he murmured as he stood in front of its roughhewn frame.

Francis scanned the crowd and saw that no one noticed them, while Jonnie focused on something several yards away. "We've got company, Mr. Holmes. There are several men dressed like those who chased us this morning heading this way."

Francis had been searching the other end of the tunnel and said, "There is another group heading toward us from the other direction as well. Whatever you do, do quickly, Sherlock!"

Holmes knew that the door would not have a key or knob and that the only way a person could pass through a fairy door was if they knew the password. He racked his brain, pushing his thoughts back to his conversation with the woman in his dream. What did she say or imply? What disguised riddle or obvious key did she leave him? She told him to come find her, so obviously she knew he would have to pass through a door. And the door would require a password.

"They are getting closer, Mr. Holmes, and it's a bit hard for me to hide." Francis groaned as he slipped to his knees and crouched low. He was as difficult to hide as a water buffalo at Tiffany's. "Huuurryy!" he half whispered. Jonnie bent behind her huge husband, and together they were as inconspicuous as a large boulder in the middle of a small stream. Holmes narrowed his eyes, then laughed as he leaned into the door and exhaled on it. In a heartbeat the wood disappeared, and he and the Alpartses tumbled in. The door quickly reappeared behind them. The converging teams met and stood right where Holmes and company had been seconds before.

Jonnie grabbed Francis and held him close as their heartbeats calmed. They were standing in the arch of an ancient stone doorway trimmed in ivy.

When the door opened, Holmes had stumbled, landing on his knees. As he picked himself up, he laughed. "Clever! She told me to breathe upon her door... and that is exactly what I did and here we are." He was still chuckling as he started down the long gaslit hallway. The Alpartses walked a few paces behind, stopping occasionally to touch the stuccoed walls of the tunnel, sensing through the tips of their fingers for the vibrations of stealthy creatures moving to meet them. The fragrance of lavender laced the air. After one such stop, they hurried to catch up to Holmes, only to discover he had also paused. The deep growl of a very large dog echoed off the cobblestone walls.

Francis looked at the animal, sniffed the air, and chuckled. "Now I understand what your invisible friend was afraid of... and what ripped him up. He ran into this wee beastie."

Holmes' eyes bulged, but he clamped his jaw shut at Francis' *wee beastie* understatement.

Standing in front of Holmes, hair raised all along its spine, was the largest doglike predator Sherlock Holmes had ever seen. He recognized the breed as an Irish wolfhound, one of the oldest breeds of dogs on the planet. The animal was huge, its hackles raised and its golden eyes narrowed.

Had Holmes been in a deductive frame of mind he would have noted that this individual broke all records for mass and height of its breed. The wolfhound was at least four and a half feet tall at its shoulder, its head about six feet.

It was easily over three hundred pounds, and covered with coarse black hair. Holmes got a very intimate view of its razor-sharp, dagger-like fangs because its lips curled back to show him.

"Don't let it see that you are afraid..." Jonnie whispered. "You wouldn't want to provoke it."

"Absolutely not! No provoking... at all." Holmes' breathing was rapid but starting to calm as he forced himself to practice deep cleansing breaths. "Did I happen to mention that I don't like big dogs and have not since the Baskerville incident?"

Francis edged forward, trying to get between Holmes and the dog. "No, sir, I don't think you did." He raised his open rock-hard hands toward the beast, then offered one fist to the dog to sniff, all the while gently speaking to it.

Francis knew not to look the dog in the eye, thus avoiding its threatening gaze. He also knew not to smile showing his teeth. But he struggled to keep the beast in him that loved battle from breaking out its own fangs. The large man sensed that this animal was extremely intelligent... and confused. It had not expected a massive predator to come waltzing down the tunnel.

The human beast, Francis, instinctively knew alpha behavior and realized the big guy in front of him was the primary alpha of his kind. And he was not inclined to allow them to pass. But Francis wanted to pass, and the part of him that had learned civilization under the gentle hand of his wife was in the way. So, he took it off like a member of the stodgy Diogenes Club would a dinner jacket. He lifted his eyes and stared straight into the cold, narrowed eyes of the beast. The huge animal tensed and crouched, ready to spring, its rumbling growl increasing in volume.

Francis continued to press the dog, pushing it to fight or flee. He curled his lips into an exaggerated smile, baring his very large and white teeth. The huge brute stiffened, tensing on the verge of decision. Life and death edged closer. Every hair on the dog's back stood erect. Little by little Francis raised his arms, expanding his already massive profile till it filled the tunnel. The dog stepped back a fraction. Francis began to growl, a low rumbling snarl that started quietly and gradually increased in volume. The dog took another step back, and Francis moved forward, his growl decreasing just a hair. The wolfhound knew it had only one recourse; it tucked its head, whimpered, and rolled over on its back. Francis and Jonnie both eased forward to pet it, then scratched its belly. Jonnie found the tender spot behind its ears, and soon the animal was moaning in delight as she cooed to it.

"Mr. Holmes, it would be a good idea if you would move forward now, allow this big fellow to sniff you, and then scratch its belly and rub behind its ears," she said.

Holmes swallowed a large lump in his throat and started to do as Jonnie asked. The dog growled. Jonnie barked a quick "No!" and swatted its muzzle. It whimpered and hushed.

Sherlock wiped the moisture off his forehead and forced a smile to his lips that never quite made it to his eyes. But as he drew close to the huge wolf-like creature, he discovered he was enjoying the magnificent brute's strength and charm.

Holmes proceeded to let the animal sniff him, then scratched its head. He was surprised that as he did, his own heart rate eased and he delighted in the process.

Francis explained, "This dog is enchanted. It is a guardian but also a companion, and as a result emits pheromones that produce a calming effect on those who stroke it and it deems as friends. Apparently, you have been accepted, Mr. Holmes."

The creature must have reciprocated because it licked Holmes right across the face, its tongue so massive that it left behind a huge stream of dog slobber. Holmes shook his head, disgusted, and wiped the slobber off with his jacket sleeve. "Now that we have conquered this fine fellow, we should get back to our original quest."

A female voice answered from the gloom of the hall. "I think that has been achieved, Mr. Holmes." The woman who had visited Holmes in his dreams stood in front of them. Her snow-white curly tresses framed her beautiful face. Her dark-green eyes narrowed as she looked with disgust at the huge wolfhound lying on its back, legs spread and tummy up, getting scratched by Jonnie Alparts. She turned her gaze on Holmes and snarled, "But do not think I will submit to your advances as easily as this big idiot." She nudged the dog with her foot. He whimpered, embarrassed, but didn't stop Jonnie from scratching him.

The queen shook her head, barely hiding the smile threatening to curl up the edges of her lips. "Come along. We have a lot to discuss, and not long to do it. Your queen's special troops will find you soon, and when they do, they will not be nearly as agreeable."

******

Dr. Watson paced. One minute he was refraining from turning the air blue for Marie's sake and the next he was apologizing for ripping the atmosphere with vile yet colorful expletives that manifested as memories of his time in the British military.

"I guess you know you have come up in the world when you find yourself incarcerated in the Tower of London. I never thought I would see the day; I was confident Sherlock would find a way, but never me. In a bloody awful sense this is an accomplishment."

Marie caught herself from answering, but Watson had apprenticed under Sherlock Holmes and saw her hesitation. "What is it, dear? We are all friends here, and if not before, our internment surely must have contributed in some measure to a bond."

Marie drew in a frustrated breath. "You're right, Dr. Watson, but some things are better left... unturned."

Watson frowned. "I fail to grasp your meaning."

Thomas jerked his head in Marie's direction as he slid down the cold stone wall and sat on the floor. "What my dear and precious and beautiful wife is trying to avoid saying, John, is this is not her first trip or her first overnight stay at the tower."

Marie's back stiffened as she looked at her grinning husband. She didn't know whether to join his laughter or scold him. She wanted to ask, *How did you know that?*

He answered her unspoken question. "Because, my dear, I read your file. It is very large and full of speculation, and goes back over a hundred and seven years."

A breath exploded from her mouth. "What! How long—when did you read—"

"Before we ever met. It was my job to discover a way to stop the Masters' greatest agent. And I did."

"Hmmph! I don't recall you ever thwarting any of my plans or assignments," she grumbled, her pride starting to rise. *The next thing that hard-headed, arrogant beast will do is ask me my age,* she thought.

Thomas picked himself up off the floor and stepped toward his wife. Her arms were crossed over her chest. She was not looking at him. Gently he put his hand under her chin and nudged it up. She still wouldn't make eye contact. Now he knew how much she despised her past and how tactless he had been to bring it up. "That was thoughtless and cruel of me. I would rather take a beating than hurt you."

"Hmmph. That could be arranged," she murmured, but not wholeheartedly.

He continued, "I was oblivious."

"And inconsiderate," she added.

"Yes," he agreed.

"And unfeeling." She piled on the guilt, but her eyes had begun to twinkle.

He reached his arms around her, drawing him to her. "Yes," he agreed again.

"And you lied."

"How is that?" he grumbled, stepping back the smallest bit.

"You never thwarted one of my assignments." She stared up at him with a *see, I told you so* look.

Thomas Spurgeon snorted. "Yes, I did!" Then he looked down on the love of his life and, before she could retort, he kissed her. Watson turned away, smirking and red-faced.

When the kiss broke and before Marie caught her breath, Spurgeon said, "I did stop you, Marie, by using the most brilliant tactic I could devise. I married you!"

After she swatted his muscled chest and before the argument could resurge, they heard a voice.

"It's not that I mean to pry on such sweet conversation, but if I recall correctly you were going to investigate the matter of our incarceration in these dank walls. My assumption is you are still involved in said reconnoiter?" The tall man with the roguish look and muddy cape stood in front of them. This time even Watson could see him.

"By Jove!" Watson cried and choked back the rest of his exclamation.

"Yes, and you must be the famous Dr. John Watson. I have heard of you and, to be honest, expected to meet you sooner. I am surprised your exploits have not led to your incarceration before now."

Watson blinked and then bowed to the man's charm. "Thank you, sir." A new thought struck him, causing a doubtful scowl to form. "I think."

A cold wind blew out of nowhere, causing the living people in the cell to shudder. Marie drew her shawl closer and said, "I believe you have brought your friends. And to answer your question, well, we must ask our own. And if you and those with you..." She nodded to the pale-grey specters who crowded the cell and now bunched up outside the bars.

Thomas moved toward the cell gate and looked at the lines. They came from two directions. "So many!" he gasped.

"If memory serves me correctly and it does, because I looked it up before we left the flat, close to four hundred people have lost their lives here," Watson added.

"Dr. Watson, you are correct, but not all of that number has been retained here," a woman's regal voice said. Watson turned from looking down the hall at the long grey lines and saw a slender young woman dressed in elegant robes standing before him. "I am Lady Jane Grey, and this handsome rogue, who in typical rude fashion has forgone introductions, is the infamous Sir Walter Raleigh."

"My pleasure, ma'am!" Watson bowed.

"Now, Jane, you could have gone all day without skewing things with introductions. All that the people of this time remember about me is the name fits well on large dogs. One of the twins told me he looked in on a dog show, of all things, and that I should be well and goodly proud because both of the champion dogs were named for me. Walter was the name of a huge Great Dane, and Raleigh some big chunk of wolf."

Thomas snorted and was about to ask Marie how they were supposed to interview four hundred ghosts when Lady Jane spoke. "Thomas Spurgeon, well and good it is to meet you. We have heard of your exploits even in this stone cage. To answer your question, four hundred are not incarcerated. There are only forty-four of us. Just those you see forming lines along this hall. That is it. The rest were able to move on almost immediately after their deaths. We are those that remain. And wish we didn't."

Watson looked at Thomas and then Marie. "What is the common theme presenting upon this dreaded host? Like a disease it has manifestations, and like a crime it leaves clues. And apparently it is our lot to ask and discover."

Six hours later...

Watson had slid down the stone wall and was barely moving. Marie had snuggled into the corner and covered herself with a threadbare blanket left by their jailer. And Thomas lay on his back in the middle of the floor, staring at the ceiling.

Sir Walter Raleigh paced between the cell and the hall, flowing through the iron bars at will. He stopped on occasion to peer down on Thomas or frown at Watson. Once he stopped and grumbled, "The spirit is indeed willing but the flesh is weak. But bloody Hades, man, we've been stuck in this limbo for centuries. Was there not some type of illumination that crept its way into your heart after hearing all those testimonies?"

Thomas turned to Marie, catching her look and slight nod. He slowly sat up and slid back until he was braced against the wall. "Sir Walter, you saw what we did. You heard what we heard. What intrigues me and baffles me, sir, is that you did not understand what we realized halfway through these interrogations."

"And what is that, man? You're right, I am clueless. As is every person in this tower. What is the answer?"

Marie whispered, "Dear sir, I am afraid you will not like it... but the patterns are obvious, and the conclusion resolute. I am reminded of one of your famous authors—Dickens was his name. He had one of his nefarious characters say, 'I wear the chain I forged in life, I made it link by link, and yard by yard; I girded it on of my own free will, and of my own free will I wore it.'"

"What the bloody hell does that mean?" Raleigh's screech caused the temperature in the cell to drop even further. He glared down on the exhausted trio; his eyes lit with angry passion. Then he felt a gentle hand on his wrist and another on his shoulder. The air inside the cell warmed. Lady Jane and several other pale visitors had gathered around the old pirate; their touch consoled him. His breathing, if you could call it that, calmed, and his heart, had he a heart, stopped racing.

Dr. Watson was visibly roused and stood to his feet. He raised a gnarled finger at Raleigh and scolded, "Do not blame these children for being honest. And do not hold against them your own sins, the chains of your own forging. There is a way out, sir. There always has been, but you have been loath to take it, and so in your intensity have conveniently forgotten the means of your own freedom."

Thomas and Marie stared wide-eyed as Watson levied his pale audience. They were pleasantly surprised at Dr. Watson's oratorical ability but shouldn't have been. There were reasons he was Sherlock Holmes' right arm.

"You walk these halls because of injustice, and that is widely known. But the tormentors that hold you here do so not because of what was done to you but because of what you refuse to release. Matthew 18:21, sir, note your Bible. You are the key to your own chains, sirs and madams." He turned to the crowd of apparitions listening to him. "Release those who unjustly bound you, who persecuted you without cause. Who falsely accused you and even... stole your life away from you? Forgive them and be freed from them."

A door creaked open down the stone hallway, and the spirits vanished. Keys jingled, and Watson and his associates waited, watching the iron bars. A large and familiar face appeared, accompanied by a guard.

Mycroft Holmes looked at Watson and signaled the guard to unlock the cell. "I don't know whom you were addressing, Doctor, but I do have a question. Have you ever considered standing for Parliament? You are an outstanding orator. And you have a visitor. I tried to dissuade her from accompanying me but... well, you will see."

******

Holmes and the Alpartses followed the queen down the gaslit hall to a wrought iron door. She waved her arm across it and the door opened, shrieking on its hinges. Bright rays like morning in a spring forest broke through the doorway. Along with it came warm breezes and the smell of pine trees and fragrant bee balm mixed with spearmint and lavender. As they stepped across the threshold, the sound of a hermit thrush and redbird holding a concert met them as honeybees provided the background thrum.

The queen spread her arms, encompassing the view before them. "Welcome to my kingdom. Nothing here will harm you unless you seek to harm this world or mar its beauty. You may eat anything served you without fear. And none of my subjects will attempt to entice or bargain with you. Do not worry; you will make no deals with the devil in this land, although his negotiating skills might be useful later."

Holmes scowled but the Alpartses paid no notice. They were awestruck. The land was blessed, and they had the strongest desire to take off their shoes and traipse barefoot across it. But Holmes was set on his objective and knew time could pass quickly. "I know we would all like to enjoy your wonderful kingdom..." He wanted to call her by name but realized he had no idea what her name was.

A twinkle lit her eyes. "What would you like to call me, Sherlock Holmes? Would Mabe work for you? Or Magdalene? What of Shariel? Would that do? You know names are important. I have not shared mine because I do not care to be summoned. But you are my guests and you must call me something, so let it be Shariel... yes, that will do... for the time being. Now what do you want to know? Before you ask, I answer thee, the diamond is home. It cannot leave this place nor can it be stolen again. So, where that leaves you, I do not know."

Queen Shariel led them to a table spread with all types of delights—meats, pastries, fruits, and the most delicious-smelling vegetables. "Here, let us eat and discuss these matters as we do."

Holmes was not inclined to be distracted and felt convinced the fairy was doing her best to sidetrack him, which fairies were wont to do. But England wasn't fond of

The Long Game

bulldogs for nothing, and when his ire arose Sherlock Holmes was a bulldog.

"Queen Shariel, you know the dilemma I find myself in: caught as it were between two queens. It might help if you were to enlighten me on the legal right you claim as original owner of the diamond. I would hope that were you able to substantiate that claim, the empire would feel a moral obligation to abide by your rightful ownership. Either we are a land of law or one of anarchy led by the powerful who consider themselves above that which anchors us all. I acknowledge you are under no compulsion to provide any evidence other than your own good word. However, I also know that fairies have honor and would wish to avoid innocent bloodshed if at all possible."

"Innocent Mr. Holmes. Your patriarchs are some of the vilest scum ever spawned on this planet. You have waged wars and changed religions simply because of a sovereign's selfish lusts. Why should I humble myself to provide any substance other than my word to such as that?"

Holmes was prepared for that reply and answered simply, "Because, madam, you are not like them. And that is the position many of them would take."

Shariel smirked and then nodded. "Mr. Holmes, even after I share the history of the diamond, what evidence will you have that what I am telling you is true? How shall I prove my testimony? What is the word of one sovereign to another if no one believes either of them?"

Holmes grimaced. This time he was caught flatfooted. He gulped, took a sip of wine, and scrubbed his brain for an answer.

Then Francis spoke. "Would the word of the one who stole the diamond in the first place suffice?"

Every head at the table turned toward him. He continued, "Jack Griffin is here."

Holmes started, as did the queen's guards. Francis went on, "He tried to sneak by us when the dog stopped us. But I scented him, as did Jonnie. We thought it better to wait and see what he was up to. But as I listened to your conversation with Queen Shariel, it occurred to me that if anyone could prove the diamond was stolen, it would be the thief that stole it. But, sir, I am also just now aware that he has gone back to the door to lead Queen Victoria's troops here. We do not have long to dally."

Shariel jumped to her feet and barked orders to her warriors, and just like that they disappeared. Holmes heard the rustle of their leaving and realized the English special forces that followed him were in for a very rude reception. He nodded and then walked over to the queen and knelt.

The act took her by surprise. She ceased giving orders and beckoned him to rise. "You have my attention, Sherlock Holmes. What is it you wish to say?"

******

Watson heard the shuffle of a long dress and the clicks of several boots on the stone floor of the tower hall. Mycroft turned toward the sound, bowed, and stepped away from the cell door.

The cell door opened and a short, dumpy woman dressed in dark colors looked at him. Watson stuttered, wide-eyed, and then bowed from the waist. Thomas Spurgeon's eyes also widened, and he too bowed low. Then Queen Victoria looked at Marie, and this time her eyes were the ones to blink. A hand covered her mouth and her head shook disbelievingly. "Mein Gott!" she whispered. "Is it really you?" She stepped toward Marie, her hands outstretched, her fingers reaching. A soft smile lit on Marie's face as the queen of England gently touched her cheek.

"It's good to see you, Drina. You are looking well," Marie whispered.

"How? You haven't aged. I am an old woman and you were my nursemaid. You raised me. And now here you are."

"You knew who I was. But I guess when you see it up close it can be a little unsettling."

Victoria shook her head and whispered, "That, my dear Marie, is an understatement."

With a final shake of her head, Victoria turned back to Watson and Thomas. "Gentlemen, I am not disposed to apologize for subordinates' behavior, but if I were, I would. Having said that, let me ask you: has there been any progress on the theft of my diamond?"

Thomas looked at Watson, who reddened, then said, "We have made some interesting discoveries, Your Majesty. And they all seem to indicate there is more here than a theft of the diamond."

A cold breeze blew through the cell, catching the queen and her guard unawares. Marie's eyes lost focus and she covered her mouth, whispered to an unseen person at her side, then sighed and addressed the queen. "Victoria, would you be open to another individual's perspective on the developments of this, ah... situation?"

Victoria grew suspicious. "I see only three persons in this room, Marie. Whose perspective might you be suggesting?"

The translucent form of the bearded rogue Sir Walter Raleigh, this time his cape cleaned and his boots polished, appeared before the queen. He looked down on her and said, "I believe, Vicky, that she was referring to me!"

To her credit the queen did not faint or cry out. She did pale and her hands trembled, but she mastered her fear and kept it from her voice. "And who, sir, might you be?" Then her eyes narrowed and a smile of recognition broke across her face. "Sir Walter Raleigh? Are you really Sir Walter?"

The fact that the queen of England remembered him and was thrilled to meet him touched the old pirate's heart. He bowed deeply before her. "Forgive my familiarity, my lady. I have been out of polite society for quite some time and forgot my upbringing."

All semblance of fear left Victoria and she giggled. "Amazing. Absolutely amazing!" Then she went where Marie knew she would. "Sir Walter, do you know my dear Albert? Are you able to communicate with him?"

The hope on her face caused the ghost to frown and release a deep sigh. "No, my queen, I have never met him. You see, ma'am, he did not suffer the same fate as most of us trapped here in the tower. He met his end naturally; I, on the other hand, was..." He drew a finger across his neck.

She gulped, noticing the thin red scar that encircled his fine head. "I see. Well then..." The moment stretched longer than anyone felt comfortable with. Victoria was noted for bouts of uncontrollable grief. But this time she wrestled with her darkness and won. "Sir Walter, Marie said you shared a unique perspective?"

"Aye, madam, I do. I saw the thief take the diamond. And, ma'am, did you note something strange? The thief did not seize the other jewels, although they were hers for the taking. Does that not strike you as odd?"

Victoria stiffened, and Holmes' crew noticed it immediately.

"I had not considered it such, Sir Walter. I mean, the largest diamond in the world was surely enough?"

"Really, ma'am? You would not have made a very good pirate, and I would have had to counsel you in the ways of good thievery."

She rolled her eyes. Had there been others of her guard in earshot she would have taken offense, but Walter Raleigh was a charmer, and it wasn't in her to scowl at him, just yet.

"Do you think, good lady, considering all the Christian virtues we are called to and your office represents, that perhaps there was another motive behind the theft of the one diamond and the leaving of the rest?" Sir Walter watched Victoria's features, realizing he was in a duel and out of practice, while she endured and sharpened her wits daily.

"None that I can think of, sir. What do you suggest?"

Raleigh smirked. "Really, ma'am? I realize I am just a poor wraith, but I also know that eternity waits for us and judgment is horrible, ma'am. It doesn't boil; it simmers, and I have endured it for two centuries. That is a very long time to give thought, my queen, and... I do not wish it on another."

Victoria's ire was rising. Her cheeks had reddened and her eyelids fluttered.

Thomas sought to intervene. "Your Majesty, please forgive Sir Walter. He does not realize the insult."

"Oh, but I damn well do, boy! And better yet, I realize the insults and offenses of this entire empire better than most. We have lied and betrayed and murdered and stolen our way through time, and the reason we rule is not because of divine pronouncement but because we are better at thievery than most, and I have been paying for it through the nose!" He pointed to the queen. "And this woman knows the truth. She has access to the private histories and the journals, and knows that of which I speak, but what she doesn't realize is the price is high. It is so high!" he screeched like the old-fashioned banshee he was. "And I am trying with all that lies within me to spare her that!" He turned back to her, her color drained by his ghostly wail.

"Woman, you know that diamond does not belong to England. You know Jack Griffin stole it from the fairies and gave it to Thomas Cullinan, who saw to it that the Transvaal Colony government, which, by the way, is brimming with insurrection and scoundrels, would use it to bribe you into showing them favor." He turned back to Thomas and continued his tirade. "She is trading her influence for a sparkly and doesn't realize it."

"You're wrong! You may be an ancient old wisp, but you have no idea what you are talking about! The colony was proud to bestow upon the crown that remarkable jewel!"

"Milady, think. Do you know how they got hold of the diamond? Do you know why the thief, who was a fairy, by the way, left all the other jewels? Do you know why the Masters have sent a small army in your name to invade that mystical kingdom and take it back? It's power, ma'am, pure and simple, and they think you a simpleton easily manipulated and deceived."

Mycroft Holmes had heard Victoria's shouts and lumbered back to the cell. She turned to him. "Mycroft, what do you know of this? Is there any truth to it?"

He paused, scratched his jowled chin, then slowly said, "I do not know, my queen, but I know how to find out."

"See to it then!"

Mycroft bowed and then waddled away at a fast pace down the stone hallway. Victoria turned back to Sir Walter. "We are not amused! We are not amused at the accusations you have made concerning the empire. We are not amused at the insinuations that I knew of any thievery, and most of all we are not amused that you think anyone, whether they call themselves masters or maids, could manipulate my person!"

* * * * * *

"We need to talk, Queen Shariel, before your warriors shed blood. There are forces at work here that have deceived you and England's queen. And before this teapot becomes a tempest, let me parley with them."

"Sherlock Holmes, I sense that there is good intention in you, and I am well acquainted with the malicious greed for power that drives the Masters."

Holmes jerked with surprise but the queen did not stop. "Yes, Sherlock, their maleficence is well known. But I also do not want bloodshed in this land or the poison of iron unleashed to violate our ground. So, go forth and parley. But be wary." Worry lined her forehead and, in a soft voice only he could hear, she added, "Be careful, my friend."

Holmes rose, motioned toward Francis and Jonnie to follow him, and hurried down the path that led to the portal to the queen's kingdom. The huge dog followed Jonnie.

"You're not going to do anything foolish, are you, Mr. Holmes?" Francis couldn't keep the concern out of his voice.

Before Holmes could answer, Jonnie butted in, "Of course he is. He's Sherlock Holmes, first into battle, last out, and all that sort of blarney."

"Hush, woman! Don't lessen courage when so few men can wield it," Francis barked.

Jonnie was not inclined to heed such a stiff rebuke, but she did suddenly remember her husband wasn't always an emasculated civilized man and had been known to remind her on occasion.

He stopped walking and turned to her. "I am sorry, my love, please forgive me. I should not have been so quick to judge."

She responded by grabbing his hand and holding it to her lips. The beast was learning.

Sherlock Holmes stepped into the clearing that stood between the tunnel entrance and the forest of the beautiful land. He was surprised by the amount of men pouring through the gates. They were uniformed, but not in the traditional red of the British Army. They wore dark, mottled greenish-grey uniforms that blended in with the greenery around them. The men carried repeaters, and Holmes even noticed a few of the new Maxim guns had been rolled in.

Holmes wrapped his handkerchief around a stick, preparing to approach the troops. Francis wanted to go with him. "Surely, sir, you have to let me accompany you. At the very least my presence will ensure civility, and at the worst I may be able to strike down a treacherous blow before it reaches you."

Holmes heard the concern in the big man's voice and saw the fear in his eyes. "Francis, you would do those things, no doubt, but in the worst case you would also make a very large target, and if I were so unlucky as to survive such a blow and brought you back bullet-riddled, upon whom do you think Jonnie would take out her wrath? Hmm?"

The huge man smirked and nodded, then reached out his hand. "Good luck, sir, and may God go with you!"

Holmes walked forward with a white flag in his hand.

An officer noticed him and immediately signaled the men in his command not to fire. The troops continued to pour in and spread out before the entrance to the tunnel. Holmes was not at all sure that Shariel's warriors would be able to hold these forces back.

The officer dressed in the uniform of a Ranger major strode out to meet Holmes. He was tall and well built, wearing traditional muttonchops and holding himself with supreme confidence. "You, sir, are under arrest!" he barked as he strolled up to Holmes. "You have aided and abetted the thieves involved in the theft of Her Majesty's diamond."

Holmes spoke calmly. "Sir, I am here under a white flag. I came to negotiate an agreement with a falsely accused people on Her Majesty's behalf."

The officer chewed on that for the briefest of moments, then answered, "Mr. Holmes, your reputation precedes you, and for that and the assistance you have given to the crown on many occasions I respect your right to parley. However, sir, on the substance of your claim I am unauthorized to comment and must insist on your surrender and that you and any associates that may be with you, along with the stolen gem, accompany me."

Holmes' keen eye had noticed that the man was not a regular British Army officer. "Sir, since you are not in the service of the queen but in the employ of an undesignated company, I must respectfully decline."

The officer's eyes narrowed. His face hardened and he moved for the six-barreled derringer at his side.

Three things happened at once. The man's hand suddenly flew loose from his arm, blood squirting like an undisciplined fire hose. A rain of arrows thundered down on the troops storming through the tunnel gate, and Sherlock Holmes vanished.

The major crumpled to the ground face-first. Others screamed as arrows pierced them, but apparently the leaders who had sent them to invade had prepared for such an event. The men wore armor made from layered silk for protection against projectiles. It was known to stop arrows, so not as many fell as the fairy warriors had hoped. Then the Maxim guns opened and the repeating guns of the Masters' army belched flame. The warriors of the queen started dying.

Fairy blood wasn't as bright as human blood, but it had the same sweet metallic smell. The queen had not prepared for war against modern weapons. Her warriors were courageous, but when courage met bullets, bullets prevailed.

Her army drew back into the forest, leaving its dead behind. Holmes hadn't realized he was invisible till the queen pulled back the veil that hid him. She had covered him and snatched him out of the battle fray before the Maxim guns thundered. Together they hid behind some large hardwood trees and gathered their breath as they listened to bullets ripping by at supersonic speeds. Her beautiful land was being ravaged, and the sweet smells that had greeted him that morning were now replaced by the stench of broken men and blood.

"Your queen betrayed me, Sherlock Holmes! She has invaded the last pristine and undefiled land upon this planet and—"

Holmes had to almost shout over the battle and the screams of Shariel. "Those soldiers are not from the queen of England. They do not even wear British uniforms or use British weapons. They are from the Masters, Shariel. The queen doesn't know they're here, and certainly would not sanction this invasion."

"But you are not sure. I read minds, Mr. Holmes. You are praying and hoping that your faith in that stumpy old grump is not unfounded."

Homes grimaced and nodded.

Francis came plowing through the woods with Jonnie and her new wolf pet loping along behind her. "We can't hold here, Mr. Holmes. We must pull back and trade ground for tactical advantage. The warriors are good fighters, but their great skill and passion is not enough. The

Masters brought an army equipped with some of the most sophisticated arms I have ever seen."

"I will not give an inch to those pigs, not an inch. We will not fall back!" Shariel screamed.

Holmes grabbed her, holding her in a frantic embrace to keep her from rushing toward the sound of battle. "Are you not willing to trade your pride for your warriors' blood, Queen? Francis is right; there are places in your land to lose this battle and places to win it, and this place," he glanced quickly around him, "is indefensible. Please, my queen, consider this giant man's wisdom." Holmes could feel her heart racing against his own as he held her tight. She was strong but he was unwilling to let her rush to her death.

"They're dying, Holmes. Can't you hear their screams?" she whispered as hot tears streamed down her face and melded with those already on his cheeks.

"And if you run headlong to them, all of them will die, as will you. Lead them, Shariel! Lead them fiercely, lead them passionately, but lead them wisely." Holmes felt her body relax and her breaths come easier.

"My queen?" she whispered, causing him to realize what he had said. "You can let me go now." Holmes loosened his grip and she pulled back, staring at him, her eyebrows arched in an expression he could not pierce. Then she turned to Francis.

"Francis Alparts, what do you suggest? Where is the best place to destroy this invasion army? And how does a monster come by this knowledge?"

Francis sighed but did not allow the word *monster* to trouble him. "I learned from a corporal, ma'am, or at least he was only a corporal when I first met him. The Little Corporal, they called him, but he conquered the world for a season."

Holmes looked at Francis, startled. The big man shrugged and then moved off to find the warriors and guide them to more defensible ground.

Just then a wounded fairy warrior limped back from the front lines, bleeding and barely able to walk. In his hands was a gold-handled sword made from a solid white stone, trimmed with silver, with its razor edge made from diamond. The tall, lean man fell at Shariel's feet. He lifted the sword to her, holding it lengthwise.

She looked on her warrior, a question behind her sad eyes.

"He fell, milady, holding back a charge so the rest of us could pull back. We are willing to die for you and the blessed land, my queen, and as soon as you have received this sword I will march back and fight as long as I can."

Shariel stared at the sword, unmoving, her eyes fixed on memories of the one who had held it for her for so long. Shots rang out and screams drew closer.

Holmes put his hand on her arm and whispered, "Shariel. We need to go."

She turned to him, tears glistening in her eyes. "Yes... but I have to do something else first."

"Well, hurry it up, ma'am." Holmes yiked as another bullet whipped through the foliage.

"Kneel, Sherlock Holmes."

"What?" he balked. "Now is not the time. We need to move back."

"Now is all the time," she answered. He frowned, puzzled. "I will explain later. Kneel," she repeated, pleading. "Please, it is the tradition of my people. It holds us together; it is part of what holds this land together. Kneel."

Holmes sighed and hit the ground, staring up at the queen. Her hair was tossed, her eyes red, her face darkened from gunpowder, but she was also amazingly beautiful. Even with bullets flying and men screaming.

"I will shorten the ceremony."

He nodded his head quickly, signaling agreement.

She continued, "Will you take this sword and all it bestows and will you pledge to honor this land and its queen till death do you part?"

"What?" Jonnie and Francis stared at the queen. Then Jonnie and a second later Francis understood and knelt. Holmes remained clueless but was willing to do whatever he had to do to remove the queen from the fighting.

"Yes, I do. I will, most certainly."

She handed him the sword. He stood, and as he did, he gripped the pommel. Energy flowed through him, power and strength like fire, agonizing and purifying. He tried to drop it, to sling it away, but he could not pry his burning fingers off it. Finally, the energy slowed and he could budge his fingers. He was about to complain when soldiers came storming through the trees, shouting and firing. Francis tried to jump in front of Holmes and Jonnie but wasn't fast enough. Holmes moved with the grace of a martial arts champion, and Jonnie like a panther.

A dozen green uniformed soldiers charged with bullets and bayonets, and in two long minutes all of them were dead. Four to Holmes' lightning-quick sword, two to Jonnie's bestial rage, and Francis just tore the others apart. The battle receded from where they stood covered with blood, and Holmes recovered his speech. "We need to move back now, milady."

Francis tilted his head, listening. An instant later Jonnie joined him, and then the wolfhound and the queen and finally Sherlock Holmes heard a different kind of rifle fire and British regulation trumpets as they echoed across the battlefield. After a moment a hush settled over the smoke-filled land.

Negotiations...

The click of boots echoed down the stone hallway of the tower prison. A brace of arms-men, front and back, escorted the stodgy woman dressed in perpetual black. She stopped at a large table covered in dark velvet that sat in the crown jewels display room. On the table lay two copies of a simple parchment document.

On one side of the table sat a high-backed wooden chair, on the other side its clone; at either end of the table were two smaller wooden chairs. Sherlock Holmes stood at the back of one of them. Behind him gathered Francis and Jonnie Alparts and Thomas and Marie Spurgeon, and of course Dr. John Watson. The queen of England nodded at Holmes and his entourage, then scowled and raised a sharp set of eyebrows. For anyone else her facial expression would have been equivalent to an angry scream. She stood there smoldering, her features stiff, her scowl fixed, and her body trembling.

The tower clock could be heard in the distance striking twelve. Victoria was red, embarrassed that she had been stood up by the fairy queen, whose chair remained empty.

She was about to turn away in an angry huff when suddenly, behind the high-backed chair intended for her, the queen of the fairies appeared. Her fairy warriors towered above her. Victoria's eyes bulged. She nearly pitched one of the fits for which she was infamous, but then Holmes interrupted.

"Your Majesty Queen Shariel," he motioned toward Victoria, then turned, "Victoria, Queen of England, bids you greetings." He turned back and addressed Victoria before she could regain her scowling composure. "It is considered an incredible honor, Your Majesty Queen Victoria, for a fairy queen to unveil herself before anyone, and even more so if she does it precisely on the stroke of noon."

Victoria's scowl melted. She gave Holmes a *you are so full of bovine fecal matter* look, and he pretended to cough to hide a snort. Then she positioned her rotund body in the high-backed chair, her feet barely touching the floor. "Queen Shariel, please be seated. We are honored by your presence on this notable occasion."

Shariel smiled. The room lit with the beauty of the mysterious lady as she slid her tall body into the seat assigned. Holmes followed suit and sat on the far end of the narrow table.

The seat at the other end of the table remained empty. Then the air around that chair shivered and distorted, and the atmosphere chilled as an apparition appeared. The long frame and bearded face of Sir Walter Raleigh manifested in the chair. He nodded to Victoria as host first and then to Shariel as guest. His eyes stayed on the fairy queen for a heartbeat longer than on Victoria, an act that did not go unnoticed by the queen of England, and whose face reflected it.

Raleigh's deep baritone voice began, "I am honored for the queens of England and of the beautiful land to grace my presence, as representative of those who have come before, many of whom still abide in this tower that act as witness of the event in question. We are here."

As he uttered the words, a cool wind whipped through the room, causing Holmes to reach for the parchments laid out on the table before they could be swept away. A dozen ghosts—queens and princes and one solitary German spy—abruptly appeared surrounding the table and the escorts of the queens. Victoria and Shariel had both been briefed on the ghosts' presence. Neither of them reacted in any way that would embarrass them or their kingdoms.

Holmes did not let enough time pass for awkwardness to set in and pushed on with the proceedings.

"In appreciation for the deliverance of her land from the designs of an invading army, Queen Shariel would like to make a presentation to Queen Victoria."

Holmes kept his eyes from rolling at his own words. Jonnie Alparts did not. Before her not-so-subtle action became a problem, Marie leaned into her, slid her hand quietly onto Jonnie's waist, and pinched her. Jonnie jerked but got the message.

As he spoke, Holmes continued thinking of the hours it had taken to reach the compromise that allowed Victoria to get her diamond back and Shariel not to have to admit to stealing what she considered rightfully hers.

Ten days before the proceedings...

Mrs. Hudson knocked on Holmes' door. "Mr. Holmes, seems you have a special delivery, sir." When he opened the door, she stood there, grey-headed with an apron around her waist and a smudge of flour on her cheek. "You have a letter. Came by special messenger."

The envelope was gold embossed, and in the envelope was expensive parchment. Mrs. Hudson lingered for a moment, hoping Holmes would open it in front of her. He smirked and looked back at her. "Who is it from, Mrs. Hudson?"

Unruffled and used to Holmes' snarky ways, she answered, "I'm not sure, sir, but based on the expensive stationery, I would say it was from a very wealthy person."

"You are probably right, dear lady. Thank you for bringing it up." And with that he closed the door. She huffed and stomped down the stairway, leaving him chuckling but also concerned for what lunch might contain later.

The letter was from Victoria, Queen of England.

> Mr. Sherlock Holmes, your presence is requested and commanded as Her Majesty's general agent apocrisiarius with the following responsibilities.
>
> You will act as Victoria's agent in negotiating with Shariel, Queen of the Under-Lands, regarding the restoration of the Cullinan Diamond to its rightful place in Her Majesty's treasury.
>
> Signed
> Victoria R.

Holmes threw the letter on the table and began to pace. "I can't believe that stubborn, arrogant old biddy has the audacity to demand I represent her." He had not made three rounds before there was another knock on the door. Mrs. Hudson did not announce her presence this time. Cautiously, with his hand behind his back and his grip on his revolver, he opened the door.

Shariel, the queen of the beautiful land, stood before him. She wore an everyday red dotted Swiss chiffon dress, with silk taffeta and cotton braid couture. The shape of the dress enhanced her broad shoulders, and the wide skirts accentuated her narrow waist. Her white tresses framed her beautiful face, setting off her dark-green eyes. Holmes took pride in being hard to ruffle. But his pride vanished in front of such a beauty. He stood at the door, one hand on the knob, one dangling at his side still holding the revolver. Shariel smiled and asked, "Well, Sherlock, are you going to ask me in or shoot me?"

His solid British composure rescued him. He nodded and tried desperately not to smile like a schoolboy. "Surely, ma'am, come in."

Then a chilling wisp of thought occurred to him. *She is here right on the heels of Victoria's command. Either this is a capricious act of fate or a shrewd act of manipulation.* His smile diminished considerably.

"Would you like some tea, Shariel?" He pointed to a chair and then seated himself.

She saw his struggle against her unconscious glamour and realized once again that humans were a great deal more susceptible to it than fairies. The air shifted in the room, seeming to lift. Holmes found it easier to breathe. Then she crossed her legs and said, "Have you given any considerations to the sword vow you took?"

Holmes breathed a sigh of relief. "To be honest, Queen Shariel, I have not had a great deal of time, but..." He rose from his seat and walked toward the mantel, where the sword lay wrapped in a common bath towel.

Shariel blinked, the air freezing in her lungs. She tried to speak and could only gulp, then had to guard herself from crying out.

Holmes saw her face. "I did not want such a beautiful sword to gather dust or fall into the hands of Bob, the Alpartses' boisterous child. Did I do something wrong?"

Shariel caught her breath, gathered her wits, and answered carefully, "Mr. Holmes, as the crown jewels are to Victoria, so that sword is to my people."

Holmes felt the walls crowd in. He was very glad he was alone that morning. It would have been embarrassing for his friends to see him faint or worse yet, considering the bile that was rising… Finally, fear stretching his voice, he whispered, "I did not know."

The fairy queen stared at him, then realized she was holding her own breath and answered, "Of course you could not have. We were in a battle, about to be attacked, and it was…" She searched for a word and finally settled on, "An immeasurable decision made in the spur of the moment and the heat of battle forced on both of us."

Holmes nodded, his composure returning, and rebuked himself. *What is it with this woman? I am not prone to losing my head around females, but with her I can rarely keep it. Get a hold of yourself, man!*

The fairy queen smiled and thought, *He has forgotten I can read his thoughts when I am close to him.*

Sherlock unwrapped the sword, took it in both hands, bowed his head, and presented it to the queen. "My dear Queen Shariel, I renounce any claim that my oath might have laid on this magnificent treasure. I would in no way wish to diminish its value or keep it from the person and peoples to whom it rightly belongs."

The queen stiffened as blood drained from her face. Her eyes narrowed to keep from widening, and a fierce glare etched itself solidly on her countenance.

Holmes lost patience. "Well, bloody damn, I am trying to do right by you, Shariel! What is it with queens? A man can't please them if he is courteous and tries to honor them, and he can't please them if he isn't, so what is the bloody point!" It was extremely rare for Sherlock Holmes to lose his temper, but this woman was making it a common occurrence.

Her head tilted as she read his intentions and his mind. Her scowl turned to a frown, then a pout, and finally to a thoughtful parting of her lips. "You don't understand, do you?"

Holmes dropped the sword in her lap and threw both hands in the air. "Understand what, for heaven's sake?"

As a master of negotiation, the fairy queen understood that timing was everything. She pursed her lips and stepped back in her thoughts. "Sherlock, I am sorry, this is not the time for this discussion. But we must have it soon. In the meantime, will you do me the honor of keeping the sword safe, and"—she exhaled a quick breath—"covered and out of the hands of Bob. I would hate for him to lop off a foot or destroy your furniture. We will come back to this discussion soon, but for the moment, I believe *your* queen has something else in mind."

Holmes scowled at her emphasis of the word *your*. He was not happy with it, and that pleased her.

For a moment Holmes was glad to change the subject, then grimaced as he remembered what the subject had to be changed to.

As soon as the words entered his mind, they must have also ricocheted off Shariel's. She jumped from her chair and screeched, "No! I will not return to her an object that was ours to start with and was stolen and used for a bribe! It will not happen. It cannot happen. Our kingdom is tied to that stone just as yours is to what?" She threw her hands in the air and began to pace.

Holmes thought, *Heaven forbid we ever have to pace at the same time.* She smirked and rolled her eyes at him. That is when it was driven home, with calamitous fury: she read his mind. "Will I be forced, as the novelist suggests to avoid having my thoughts pilfered every time I am with you, to wear a copper headpiece? Have you no decency?" he demanded. Her smirk changed to sadness. It occurred to him that mind reading might be an inescapable part of her even as the sense of smell was to the Alpartses, so he offered, "Can you even stop yourself from reading a mind, or is it so much a part of you that you must engage?"

"There are so many differences between your people and mine. How can this ever work?"

He thought she meant the negotiations with Victoria, and she let him.

"It can work with courtesy and respect for each other's privacy, and there is nothing so private as an individual's own mind. I am truly surprised you did not know that."

"In our culture, Sherlock Holmes, friends share. And there are no walls between us."

"You have an amazing culture, my lady. In mine we are such carnal creatures that often we hide our own thoughts from ourselves and are grateful for it. How much more so an unbridled imagination needs to be hidden from others. Do you understand?"

She nodded.

"Can you abstain from the practice?"

She let out a sad, slow sigh. "Yes, I can discipline myself from—how did you say it? Pilfering?" Then she laughed, but only to herself, and thought, *Or at least from letting you know when I do.*

He thought, *That will be the day. I shall have to invest in a copper inner lining for my deerstalker when I am around her.*

Then he changed his tone and pleaded, "Dear Queen Shariel, I have not known you long, but I have observed with great admiration your love for your people and your land. And before I say anything else, I acknowledge that you are in the right in this instance. The diamond is your property; it was stolen from you. But because of the manner it was presented to Queen Victoria and because she cannot reveal—and I do not think you would like for her to reveal—the existence of the beautiful land, she cannot walk away from this incident without the restoration of the diamond. And furthermore, you saw what a small army did to your land and warriors. Have you considered the size of the British Army? Surely the lives of your people and the beauty of your land mean more than a rock?"

Shariel stopped pacing and dropped back into the cushioned chair. She got quiet, then asked, "Does your offer of tea still hold?"

As Holmes boiled a pot of water and prepared to pour it over a bag, Shariel asked, "Have you ever had sweet iced tea?"

He frowned. "Why would anyone do that to tea? That sounds barbaric. Iced tea? Really? Where did you come up with such a notion?"

"Russia and recently Indonesia serve it all the time. I was visiting with a Russian diamond cutter once..." She grew quiet and thoughtful, and then her eyebrows rose and a smile settled on her face. She looked up at Sherlock. "I have considered your request, and I am willing, as an act of gratitude for her army's intervention in the unlawful invasion of my kingdom, to gift her the diamond, but I have one condition."

Holmes' eyes narrowed, and he hoped she was truthful about not reading his mind. "And what might that be, Queen Shariel?"

"That she allows my diamond cutters, who are without a doubt the most skillful and naturally gifted jewelers in the world, to cut the diamond into nine pieces."

Holmes' heart skipped a beat. Then his magnificent brain caught up and he set the tea down, unpoured. "Maybe... that just might work, because I know the diamond was actually scheduled to be cut. A time was being negotiated and jewelers were being vetted. Did you know that?"

Shariel didn't answer, but her forced smile answered for her. Holmes decided not to pursue the thought.

A day later... in Queen Victoria's office
"No! No! No! Absolutely not. I won't hear of it. She will restore the diamond and acknowledge that she stole it from us. A theft of that magnitude cannot just be swept under the rug, sir. A penalty must be paid."

Holmes stood in front of Queen Victoria's desk as she sat comfortably behind it. He could not help but compare the two monarchs, and kept reminding himself that he was respecting the office and not the person. He was also very grateful that Victoria could not read his mind.

"Queen Victoria, may I speak honestly without fear of reprisal?"

She huffed at the reprisal remark but nodded, then added, "But respectfully, sir; respectfully consider whom you address."

"As you know, there was a witness to the crime, and you have met him."

Victoria's eyes widened and she smiled as she remembered the meeting with Sir Walter Raleigh. "Indeed I have, sir, indeed I have. And what an amazing experience it was!"

"Then you remember his explanation to you as an eyewitness."

"I do, and I will not stand for such impertinence again. He accused me of being manipulated."

Holmes continued, "Perhaps his choice of words was inappropriate, but the question that remains is, was his accusation accurate? And do you wish to inherit upon your demise an afterlife such as his?"

"We have made up our mind, Sherlock Holmes, and we will not be persuaded otherwise. Your duty is to convince that fairy that she must bend to our will in this matter."

Sherlock Holmes bowed. "I need to recuse myself from this affair, milady, and bow to one that has more and better counsel to offer. He suggested to me that you might benefit from another audience and was content to provide it."

"Audience, Holmes?"

"His words, ma'am, not mine."

"And what sage personage has requested my presence to his audience, sir?" she demanded icily, scorn dripping from her lips.

"Sir Walter, ma'am. He asked me to inform you that he will visit you soon and take this matter up with you. Good day, ma'am."

And with that Sherlock Holmes left the queen, who blinked, mouth agape, as he walked out of the room.

That evening...

Victoria was a person of rigid schedule. Her servants remarked—behind her back, of course—that she even defecated on a schedule. So, when she had not retired for the night at her typical time, the household was concerned. When an hour passed, then another, and she was still in her office, they were disturbed and expecting war to be declared or the second coming. Finally, she called for her maids, and they escorted her to her bedchambers. She undressed and crawled under her covers. Right before she dozed off into a grumbling and aggravated sleep, she turned over and felt the touch of an ice-cold chest. Sir Walter Raleigh had climbed into her bed.

She gasped and gulped, trying to break into a scream. He stopped her with a chilly hand across her lips. "There, now, I wouldn't do that if I were you. Think about it! What are you going to tell them when they come running to your rescue? You going to say, 'Sir Walter Raleigh's naked ghost is lying with me'?

"Really, Vicky, do you think they will believe you? Or will they call for the doctors, who will report to the prime minister and then to Parliament, and then you know it will leak to the press. And ultimately you will be deposed and sent to an asylum where we..." He laughed with such a cold haunting laugh that she shivered even more. "Yes, I said *we*. I won't leave you, girl; we'll live out the rest of your days, and nights..."

The room began to spin. She gasped for breath. He pulled back his thumb and forefinger and thumped her right on the forehead. "Stop it. You are not some silly farmer's daughter fearful for her virginity. You are the bloody queen of England, and it is damn time you start acting like it." He sat up in bed. She noticed his manly chest, and he saw that she did. "Now what do you have to say for yourself?"

Her reply came out as a squeak. "What do you want from me?"

"I want you to cooperate with Sherlock Holmes. He is your kingdom's greatest champion; he has your people's interest in mind. Their best interest. Even at the risk of angering you! But I don't have anything to fear from you. I've already had my head chopped off." He put a hand on his neck and shoved. His head moved off center and threatened to fall off. Victoria squealed and he shoved it back. "This is what you will agree to, and here is why."

Her pride started to kick in; Raleigh could sense it rising.

"Woman, do you ever want to sleep again? Do you? Furthermore, do you really want the Masters to think they bested you with a silly bribe? They are playing you, Queen Victoria. Listen to me. You need the fairies. You need them more than they need you. Jack Griffin is out there, and he can make more like him, and knowing his masters, they've probably already started that process. So, what guards can protect you from an invisible assassin? Huh? How about if you had invisible guards? Like the fairies?"

She frowned, but Raleigh could see she was thinking.

"Furthermore, you will get your diamond back. They are even willing to cut it for you, and my queen, no one cuts the rocks like they do. There are no better artisans, no better cleavers than those folk. Are you aware that the best human jewelers are the ones with fairy blood?"

Her eyes widened.

"I didn't think so. So, will you cease this arrogant pretense of offended pride and act like the monarch I know you are and that your people need? Will you?"

She sat up in bed, her covers dropping. She frowned and then swayed, trying to wrap her brain around the proposal of the naked ghost in her bed. Finally, she said, "Yes, Sir Walter, I agree. We will receive the diamond from the fairy queen delivered in nine pieces as a gift for our intervention in the invasion of her land."

"Thank you, ma'am. I knew you were a fine woman of good sense." She smiled demurely. He reached over and kissed her lips, then said, "One more request, and it's not about the queen or the diamond. It's about me, but..." He stood in the bed. Her eyes widened and then he vanished; only his voice remained. "I am going to have young Sherlock Holmes deliver it. He needs the practice. But understand it is from me."

His voice faded and she was left alone in her cold bed. She fell back on her pillow, trembling and exhausted, but did not sleep well that night.

The next day...

Sherlock Holmes was surprised to receive a summons to appear before the queen. The time for the diamond ceremony was only two days away. The urgency of the meeting bothered him. He wasn't aware that his advocate had met with the queen the night before, nor was he aware of the decisions made.

The grand doors opened. A formally dressed guard escorted him right to the desk where the dumpy queen sat. She had been chatting with her personal servant John Brown, and they were giggling like two schoolchildren. When the doors opened and Holmes was escorted in, the laughter abruptly ceased. John Brown stepped back, then bowed and exited out a side door. Victoria stared holes in Holmes, but he did not waver. He smiled, bowed, and waited.

When she realized he would not be intimidated by a simple frown, she huffed and said, "All right, then. Your friend is very persuasive and visited with us last night. I found myself appreciating his arguments and have reconsidered my position. We will allow the queen of the under-lands to gift us the diamond, or should I say diamonds, as she is also permitted and has requested, in the highest manner we can request, to have the diamond cut."

Holmes breathed a sigh of relief and visibly relaxed. Victoria continued, "Sir Walter also implied that there was another subject to be discussed not involving the fairies, but that it was personal, involving him alone. And that you were aware of such and would be bringing it to our attention."

Holmes frowned and nearly said he had not heard when a whisper caught his attention. "Check your pocket,

Holmes. I left it there. And I want it read exactly like I wrote it."

The queen saw Holmes' face and recognized the hand of Walter Raleigh at work. "He is quite the rogue, is he not?" Her smile showed she was remembering something that Holmes had not been privy to.

"That he is, ma'am, and as you surmised, he is here with us but for some reason has declined to manifest." Holmes reached into his pocket and pulled out a weather-beaten piece of yellowed parchment. He started to read it, but his eyes whitened and blood drained from his face.

Victoria demanded, "Quick, tell me, what does he want?"

At the same time, he heard Raleigh rumble, "Do it, man. Let her know the price of my ransom!"

Holmes turned to where he assumed Raleigh had to be standing and grumbled, "This should be between you and her. It requires no other persons and should be a personal matter."

Victoria barked a command. "Holmes, you are my designate, my general agent apocrisiarius. I demand you read me the contents of that letter."

So, Holmes did.

Victoria's wails brought the household guards. They raced into the room, swords drawn, pistols ready to fire. Holmes had moved back several paces, and the queen was standing on her chair, fist raised to the sky, screaming. It was not the first time the household had seen her in that manner, and by the time the first guard grabbed Holmes by the shoulder, more to remove him from her reach than her from his, she had started to calm down. "Not him, you fool, the other one!"

The guards looked quickly about but saw no one. She noted the panicked expressions on their faces and then barked again, "Fine, it's fine. We are simply not amused. You may remove yourselves from our person without fear of reproach or our harm. Now go!"

When the last guard had backed out and the large doors had shut behind them, she spoke. "You know we cannot do this; it is beneath our station and our office to apologize for sins we have not even committed. This will not happen. No, it cannot happen."

Holmes was actually nodding his head agreeing with her when they both heard a voice they knew. "Vicky, you can change the words to suit you, but not the intent, and if you are unwilling, well, I have only one word for you."

Her eyes widened and her scowl hardened. Then she heard,

"John Brown."

Holmes crinkled his brow, puzzled. Then a sudden illumination struck him and he cast a glance at the queen. She looked back at him and didn't skip a beat. "Read it to me again. Perhaps if we changed a few words around, it would be suitable."

Holmes was dragged back from the exhausting memories of the last few days.

Finally, it had all come down to the moment before them. Queen Victoria graciously received the nine cut diamonds and oohed and awed as she held them in her hands. She took a diamond cutter's magnifying glass and held the diamonds one by one to her eye. "Striking work, absolutely amazing art. Your craftsmen are to be applauded, Queen Shariel." She fooled no one. Everyone present knew she was legitimizing the fact they were real diamonds. She then thanked Shariel.

Shariel laughed, which caused several questioning looks. She winked at Holmes, whispered "Later" in a tone that caused even more speculation, and disappeared with her entourage.

Sir Walter Raleigh and Queen Victoria stared at each other from across the table, each one waiting for the other's move.

Queen Victoria reached for the official-looking document in front of her, took a deep breath, and began to read, "'It has been brought to our humble attention that said personage Walter Raleigh has claimed aggrieved status.'" She looked up and paused. The old ghost's eyes brimmed with tears.

She tried to continue reading, then paused again. She put the parchment down and reached for his hand. She touched him and didn't react to the ice-cold flesh she held. "Sir Walter," her voice cracked, "I am not my kindred, and I would not have done to you the selfish and wicked thing they did. I have indeed read the private journals and the secret files of those times, and know those who perpetrated those crimes were so wrong, so arrogant. If it is any consolation to you, Elizabeth really loved you and was stricken that you were placed here, but her vanity, which she cursed herself for a hundred times, chained her to her decision as much as the iron that held you."

Walter's eyes grew wide, and large tears he had been desperately trying to hold back welled up and rolled off his face and onto the table. His lips trembled.

"Sir Walter," she continued, "I was not there, but my blood was, and the hidden guilt of my line is. So even though I balked at Sherlock Holmes' communication from you that I stand in my kindred's place and renounce their sin and ask your forgiveness, I do not balk now. Now I understand, now I grieve with you, and, sir, I pray that it will mend the bridges between us and the gulf that sits between you and Paradise. I have extended my hand, dear sir. Would you be so gracious as to accept it?"

Walter Raleigh stood, then leaned over and embraced Victoria. He wept for a moment, his body jerking, decades of anger and resentment falling off him with every tear. Then he knelt before her and looked up into her round face. "Oh, my queen, with all my heart I forgive you as their representative, and thank you for the knowledge that they regretted their sin. Thank you so much."

Victoria was holding his hands when he started to fade. His heart beat once, then twice, and he was gone. The other ghosts around him vanished as well, and soon it was just Holmes and his friends and Victoria's entourage in that great lonely hall.

Two days later...

On a delightful spring afternoon, Holmes was enjoying the lively banter of his friends and, if truth be known, his extended family. He puffed smoke like a dragon seated on his treasure but had switched from the black shag he favored to the more aromatic flavor that both Marie and Jonnie had coaxed, coerced, and finally convinced him to try. Jonnie's jibe, "If he had to smell like an old man, at least he could smell like a fragrant one rather than underpants left too long in an outhouse," was the last straw and had broken his will. Now the women hovered near and hugged him when entering the apartment.

Francis lay on his back on the floor tossing Bob into the air. The little boy would walk across his father, stand on his chest, and say, "Toss me, pops!" And then the child would find himself twisting through the air so close to the ceiling he could touch it and then fall giggling to land safely in his father's strong arms. Francis had been coaxing his little girl the toddler, Deborah, to try the flying. She would patter up his massive frame and balance, wobbly, on his chest; he would slowly reach out to grab her, wherein she would squeal, jump off him, and run away to hide in her mother's lap.

Thomas and Watson were engaged in a theological discussion concerning whether the monotheism that Akhenaten the Egyptian pharaoh had tried to install should be considered as absolute monotheism or whether it was monolatry, syncretism, or an odd mix. Jonnie, despite Deborah's interruptions, was trying to teach Marie how to knit.

The knock on the door surprised everyone. Especially the Alpartses; they could not smell anyone or hear any steps upon the stairway. Marie also jumped, focused her eyes on the door, and frowned. She couldn't sense an aura there. Francis looked to Holmes and whispered, "Should I stand in front of you, sir?" He had already handed Bob off to Jonnie, who had grabbed Deborah's little waist and rushed to the back room. Thomas deployed toward the door as well, reaching for the semi-automatic prototype pistol in his shoulder holster.

A woman's voice called from behind the door, "It's really all right, my friends... I mean no harm."

Holmes recognized the voice and moved a little quicker than normal toward the door. Marie raised an eyebrow. Jonnie had stuck her nose back in the living room and, also noticing, quickly tried to hide a grin.

Holmes straightened his rumpled shirt and opened the door. Shariel, the fairy queen of the under-lands, stood at the door in nice but common English ladies' dress. Her snow-white hair streamed down to lay on her shoulders. Her face shone with a light rarely seen on the streets of London. She looked at Holmes and said, "May I come in?"

The whole group answered at once, confusing everyone and embarrassing Jonnie and Marie. Shariel laughed and then addressed them all, "I was walking by and thought, *I wonder if Sherlock Holmes is in and if he is, if he would like to go for a walk?* That would be acceptable, would it not?" She eyed Jonnie and Marie, who both assumed a matronly protective nature toward their boss. Their broad smiles answered before Holmes could speak.

"I think I can answer for myself, thank you very much!" He reached for his jacket as he answered, in a tone that every one of the most observant and discerning humans in London standing in the room filed away for future consideration. Except Watson, who looked confused and clueless.

Holmes turned toward his friends. "Don't wait up; not sure when I will be home. I'll be fine, don't come looking for me, and... don't worry... Other than that, have a good evening." He closed the door behind him, leaving several ruffled feathers, of which he did not care one fig.

When they got to the end of the staircase, he was about to offer Shariel his arm and open the front door when she said, "Not that way," and headed for the kitchen door that opened to the small backyard, which contained a plane tree. Or had; apparently, a certain fairy queen had walked through very recently and the plane tree had grown, blossomed, and spread until it expanded into a small grove. Holmes was getting used to being astounded at the queen's antics and just shook his head, following her into the grove that seemed to close behind them and open before them until it was obvious to the consulting detective that he wasn't in London anymore.

Shariel grabbed his arm like originally intended, and together they strolled down a spring path lined by beautiful blooms that resembled sunflowers and moved to face them, then to follow them as they passed. Finally, the walkway opened into a small garden. In the garden a spring bubbled happily. Holmes knelt beside it and saw his reflection. He dipped his hand into the ice-cold water, drew back a cupful, and started to slurp it down, but, gasping, inhaled it down the wrong pipe. His eyes popped wide. Even though he was choking and Shariel was pounding him on the back, saying, "Are you all right?" his stare remained fastened on the huge diamond lying on the bottom of the spring. He looked back at her, and she answered with a mischievous smile. He reached into the spring and brought up the Cullinan Diamond. Holding it in his hand, he leaned back on the grass surrounding the spring and laughed.

"I should have known; I should have known. You gave in too easily. One minute you were adamant, then you were talking about Russian iced tea, and then it hit you—deception and twist! Brilliant. Absolutely brilliant!" He bent over laughing. "Oh, this is amazing... Victoria saves face, gets what she expected, and you get back what was rightfully yours. I am delighted. Seldom do my cases work out so well. This is superb!"

"Well, I am glad you think so, my dear Holmes. I honestly didn't think we could pull it off, but when I realized you had not discerned my little ruse, I knew there was a chance."

Holmes leaned back in the grass with no danger of small insects irritating or any type of rough cocklebur piercing his flesh. He held the diamond up to the brilliant morning sun, noting the amazing rainbow it cast.

The queen joined him by the spring, took off her sandals, and dangled her feet in the bubbling stream. "Sherlock?"

"Yes, my queen?"

"Hmm... funny you should say that, just now."

Holmes' intuition twitched, and his huge smile turned down a notch or two. "What is it, Shariel?"

"Do you remember we never finished our conversation about the sword?"

"That is correct. I have pondered your response and my carefree treatment of that precious artifact, and I apologize for my ignorance. I really had no idea. I will be happy to restore it to you."

"It belonged to the captain of my guard. He sent it back to me as he prepared to lead the charge that bought time for his warriors. He was very dear to me."

Sherlock Holmes sat up and turned to face her. "I grieve your loss, Shariel... I truly do. A good friend is a treasure greater than the greatest jewels."

"I wholeheartedly agree, dear Holmes, but he was more than a friend."

"Oh," Holmes whispered, his breath almost stopping. "A relative, a brother, a cousin?"

Her eyes locked on his as she shook her head.

"Your father?!"

A smile settled with the faintest bit of sadness; she shook her head again, never taking her eyes off him.

"Your husband?" Holmes half breathed the question.

"In my world our customs are different. In your world he would have been called my husband. And his responsibilities to me were much the same."

"Oh, my dear lady, I grieve with you at your great loss. I don't know how I would deal with such a loss; I have never known someone so intimately."

"Thank you, Sherlock. I cannot imagine such a life of emptiness. I lost but I had someone to lose. You have not lost but have had nothing to lose. Who has suffered more?"

Holmes cast a downward glance. There were no words to frame the depth of loneliness rising from the dark places he had kept for such a long time.

Shariel said, "Sherlock, are you aware that the deeper you walk in my kingdom, the more time changes? In one place time forges quickly ahead, in another it almost comes to a stop, when compared to how it behaves here."

"I was not," he answered, glad to change the subject.

"I have walked deep into my kingdom since the talks with Queen Victoria."

Holmes tilted his head slightly, his intuition once again tingling. He was not sure where the conversation was going but knew it wasn't just idle chatter.

She continued, "In your time it would have been two years."

"Really?"

"Yes, and they have been long and friendless. And now I come to the subject of the vow you took concerning the sword. I had to make a huge decision that day. Someone had to guard the sword. I cannot be sovereign and captain of the army at the same time. And whoever takes responsibility for the sword has other... obligations as well."

The hair on Holmes' neck stood on end. His heart beat faster. Gulping, he said the only thing he could think of. "Really?"

"Yes." She was treading softly but resolutely. He could sense it. "Aren't you going to ask me what they are?"

Holmes knew he had come to the point of no return. He had come to a crossroad where two paths diverged, and he knew whichever he took there would be no turning back. One of the paths was very familiar; he had walked it for years and knew every marker along its way. The other was barely trodden. He took a deep breath of the fragrant crisp air, savored it, and then slowly breathed it out. He leaned over and gently pressed his lips against the fairy queen's. "I think I know."

William David Ellis, Author

Thank you for reading *Sherlock Holmes: The Long Game.* It is the second book in the *Angels, Saints and Sinners* series. In this novel, I involve the great detective in the paranormal, but hey, his original author had a thing for that too, and it is in that vein I extended things. If you liked it, please leave me a **great review!!**

This is the second book in my Sherlock Holmes series. The first book was received well and people clamored for more. I hope you like twists and cliff hangers. I have developed a love of twists, they seep out my pores, and wake me in the night. Hopefully, you will enjoy them too.

As you read, you will discover all the familiar characters of the Holmes cannon plus more. It seems when Holmes and Watson open the door of the paranormal, they invite a host of folks in, and some of them decide to stay!

Anyway, things you might like to know: I live in the little community in East Texas where the adventures of my series, *The Harry Ferguson Chronicles*, are set. There is actually a café where my characters eat breakfast and wait on patrons. It is purported to be the most haunted house in Texas... at least it was till my people moved in. They also talk like East Texans.

Other Books by William David Ellis available on Amazon

Dragons and Romans

A Roman legion squares off against a dragon conjured by a demonized high priest of child-sacrificing Carthage. And that's what history actually records. What happens next is the action-packed tale. If you like the supernatural, action, dragons, and alternate-history fantasy with a little cussing, and a little kissing, and some horror and gut-busting tension thrown in, you will love *Dragons and Romans*, winner of the B.R.A.G Medallion.

The Princess Who forgot She Was Beautiful

WINNER OF THE READER'S FAVORITE 5 STAR REVIEW

Award-winning Novel...It started as a story...but a mysterious little girl changed everything. Now, a dragon has come to East Texas and they need a hero. An Old man rises to a glory he never thought he'd know again, and all because he was coerced into telling little kids a story. A young boy, a princess, a talking sword and an evil dragon captivate snaggled-tooth munchkins... Then the old man starts to feel it. Something has risen from his past and its coming for him and the people he loves. You'll love this first book because of the twists, turns, and even the cliff hanger ending. It will start you on a path that leads to happiness with frequent stops for humor. You won't be able to put it down. If you enjoy Fantasy, this book is for you. Get it now.

Dances with My Dragon

Harry Ferguson is a time-traveling warrior in love with a shape-shifting Dragon Princess. He has waited for her for centuries. As their lives unfold on different continents, in different ages, fighting different battles, Harry and Sarah long for a love that was timeless and the life that should have been. The second book in the Harry Ferguson Chronicles this book like its predecessor has twists at every turn and will keep readers up at night, red-eyed and caffeine braced racing through this epic fantasy. Warning: This series is a saga, and while loose ends are tied up, it isn't over until it's over! Oh My Dragon!

Kisses of My Enemy

Belle Rodum loves Harry but she's got to kill him. So... what happens when a witch who has never encountered a man she couldn't seduce or kill falls for a Dragon Rider she has to destroy?

Sarah Linscomb, a shape-shifting dragoness, loves Harry. She visits him in her dreams. But Sarah is a thousand years away, and a magnificent Berber king fighting for the survival of his people needs her. His people need her, but what does she need?

Did I mention Harry is a time traveler? Nazis are conjuring a demon to infuse their soldiers with its power. Belle is charged with protecting it. And Harry has to destroy it.

Everybody is doing the right thing and no one is happy about it! This is the third book in the Harry Ferguson Chronicles.

Get it now!

Free!

Want more? I have several short stories available on my website. Check it out.

williamdavidellisauthor.wordpress.com